Politics of Magic

Ember Academy for Young Witches, Volume 6

L.C. Mawson

Published by L.C. Mawson, 2020.

This is a work of fiction. Similarities to real people, places, or events are entirely coincidental.

POLITICS OF MAGIC

First edition. August 1, 2020.

Copyright © 2020 L.C. Mawson.

Written by L.C. Mawson.

Also by L.C. Mawson

Engineered Magic
Soulbound

Engineered Rebel
Rebel
Resist
Rebuild
Reconnect
Reconsider
Resolution
Engineered Rebel: Books 1-3
Engineered Rebel: Books 1-6
Engineered Rebel: Books 4-6

Freya Snow
Hunt
White
Wings
Oracle
Witch
Enhanced
Reaper
Trident
Kingsguard
Princess
Queen
Warden
Pandora

Separated
Healing
Family
Exiled
Torn
Prisoner
Belonging
The Royal Cleaner: Books 1-3
The Royal Cleaner: Books 1-6
The Royal Cleaner: Books 4-6
The Royal Cleaner: Books 7-9
The Royal Cleaner: Books 1-9

Table of Contents

Thank you to all of my supporters for helping me fuel my new soap-making hobby (I know that that's the same as last time, but it's still what's holding my interest...).

Special thanks go out to Seph De Busser, Peter Allan and Jo Curnoe!

Cover by MoorBooks Design.

Chapter One

S arah's sigh carried through the whole room as she reached down and grabbed her wand.

I frowned, wondering just what exactly she intended to do with it.

Especially when she'd just found out that Dana, the old leader of the Amazons, had killed Esme, the new leader and Sarah's friend and mentor.

And Willow had just announced that she was on a quest to solve the corruption that had led to Esme's death by any means necessary.

And probably involving her new assassin training.

"I should get you girls healed up so that you can rest," Sarah said with a resigned shake of her head.

I guessed Sarah wasn't the type to go on a short-sighted revenge quest.

My stomach twisted at that and I realised that I'd been hoping that she had been.

I didn't think that I could stand without aid if I tried, but... Dana had killed Esme.

And I hadn't been able to stop her.

Willow might have put an end to both Dana and Michael, but the Council had been the ones pulling their strings.

And they had to be stopped before they hurt anyone else.

Before I failed to stop them killing someone else, just like Esme and Maria before her.

Freya frowned, her words pulling me from my thoughts. "Sarah, I can take care of this. You should-"

"It's fine, Freya. It's better if I just focus on my work."

Freya nodded as Sarah looked over everyone, and very quickly settled her attention on me.

Her gaze drifted over the bite marks on my neck, and then she shifted her attention to Natalie, and the healing wound on her side.

The wound that would have been fatal if I hadn't let her drink from me, my blood accelerating her Vampiric healing.

And binding the two of us together.

Sarah sighed. "I take it Natalie had to bite you to survive?"

I nodded. "Dana snapped our wands, destroyed our healing potions and injured Natalie before locking us in a cell. I could see that the wound was going to be fatal, so..."

"Well, luckily for you, if there was no intention behind the bond, it might not be permanent."

"Wait," Natalie said, rushing over, "it's not?"

"Well, it is when you *want* to bond, but when you're just exchanging blood, with no intention or want to bond behind it, the bond that's formed isn't very strong. Time apart should break it. Though, you two are roommates, so you might need to be separated for a while."

Auntie Jess turned to Ms Griffin. "Willow may no longer be a student here, but while we deal with the current situation, it might be a good idea for her to stay in one of the guest rooms. While she does, Amy can stay with her. Assuming that's what they want."

She turned to us, and Willow nodded before turning to me.

"If that's what you want, Amelia, I'd be more than happy to stay here with you."

"Yes, it is."

Natalie turned to Sarah. "And that will break the bond?"

"If you want it broken, then there's a good chance that it will work, yes."

"Good."

My stomach twisted at the surety behind her words.

I had no idea why. I wanted this as well. We hadn't bonded because we'd wanted to, it had simply been the price of saving Natalie's life.

But still, the thought of breaking the bond unsettled me.

I pushed that thought away, though. This was what Natalie wanted, and undoubtedly what Willow wanted.

And Willow was back now, so everything between the three of us could go back to exactly how it had been before Willow had left. Willow and I could be together again, and Natalie and I could go back to being friends.

Just as soon as the bond between Natalie and me broke.

Assuming Willow actually wanted to stay with me after I'd bonded with Natalie.

And after I'd so spectacularly failed the mission and required her to save me.

Shit, did she think I was utterly useless?

Of course, she did. She'd had to save me, after all. And I couldn't even stay unbonded for her...

Willow moved over to me and took my hand, her gaze filled with concern as she looked me over.

"Are you sure that you want to stay with me?" she asked. "I mean, I know that I left, and... Things might have changed for you. If you want another room, I'm sure that that could be arranged."

I leaned forward as quickly as I could, kissing her as I desperately hoped that her words meant that she still wanted me.

That she wasn't pushing me away and tossing me aside.

Thankfully, she returned the kiss.

"I definitely want to stay with you," I said as I pulled away and a slight blush formed over Willow's cheeks.

Freya approached at that point, giving us both a firm look. "Amy, you need rest." She then turned to Willow. "I mean it, no strenuous physical activity until she's recovered. Got it?"

Willow's slight blush turned bright red, growing to encompass her entire face, and I was sure that I looked just as bad.

"I promise I'll let her rest," Willow managed, probably still reeling from the Demon Queen telling her whether or not to have sex with her girlfriend.

Because that was what we were talking about, right? And if Willow and I were sharing a room together...

Freya then turned to me with a firm look. "And don't go testing her patience, Amy. I mean it, you need sleep." She turned back to Willow. "And you had better look out for my baby sister, okay?"

"Okay. I swear, I will."

Freya nodded, seemingly happy with that as Ms Griffin indicated for Willow and me to follow her. "Come on, girls. Let's get you to one of the guest rooms."

Ms Griffin then led us to the administration building, and the guest rooms below, showing us to the one at the other end of the corridor from Freya's room.

She turned to Willow. "Do you need a change of clothes or anything?"

Willow patted a small pouch at her belt. "No, I've got everything I need here."

Ms Griffin nodded before turning to me. "I'll have everything from your room shifted here once I'm back in my office. Let me know if you need anything else."

"Thank you," I said, and she nodded before leaving.

I turned my focus to my armour, but I was so tired and light-headed that I kept fumbling with the clasps.

"Here," Willow said, leading me to sit down on the chair in the corner of the room before helping me.

"Thanks," I said, trying to help – I didn't want Willow to change her mind, to decide that I really was too useless for her to stay – though I kept getting distracted, my attention heading back to look at Willow, almost in disbelief.

She eventually turned to me with a frown as she finished with the final clasp. "Something wrong?"

I shook my head, not wanting to burden her with my anxieties.

She was here, wasn't she? So, me insisting that I didn't think she really wanted to be would just irritate her.

And then she really would leave.

No, I was being irrational, and I didn't want to scare Willow off by admitting that aloud.

"No, nothing's wrong," I said as I forced a smile. "Just... I'm so glad that you're back."

Willow smiled and I leaned forward to kiss her, the move causing my armour to fall away, leaving me in just the black under suit.

Willow pulled away, however. "You need to change. And possibly shower."

My heart constricted in my chest. Was this the sign I'd been looking for? The point where the brilliant and talented woman in front of me realised that I was just a stupid girl who couldn't save the people close to her?

No, dammit, this was Willow. She'd never thought that, she'd never been one of those people who saw me that way.

Yes, this was another failure, and every failure came with the chance that someone would change their mind. That they would see me differently.

But Willow had never seen me that way.

So, I would stay until she explicitly told me to go. And I wouldn't give her any more reason to want to leave.

I groaned, figuring that that would be so much easier if we could finally have sex or bond and I could at least give her that much. But I also knew that Willow was right about the shower, given that the parts of my skin still visible were covered in grime.

Still, I cringed at the thought of standing up for that long.

Willow seemed to understand, taking her wand and muttering a spell under her breath.

As she spoke, the spell washed over me, clearing away the blood and grime.

I sighed in relief, though there was an undercurrent of frustration as I remembered the destruction of my own wand.

And the fact that I wouldn't be able to access my magic again until I replaced it.

Not that I could risk accessing my magic when I was so exhausted.

Willow then moved over to the drawers and found my favourite pair of pyjamas that Ms Griffin must have already shifted to the room, before tossing them over to me.

I didn't even attempt to catch them, letting them fall on my lap before I pulled off my clothes.

Willow turned away as I changed, before pulling her own pyjamas from the pouch on her belt, despite the fact that the pouch looked far too small to keep them in, before getting changed herself.

I tore my gaze away, only returning it when Willow made her way back over, now in her pyjamas, and offered me her hand.

I took it as she led me over to the bed, a blush forming over my cheeks again as I climbed in on one side, and she climbed in on the other.

"I meant it before, you know," I said as I found myself unable to stop staring at her, as if she would disappear again if I dared to look away. "I'm really glad that you're back."

"I'm glad that I'm back, too."

I leaned forward, kissing her with everything I had.

I moved to straddle her, looking for a more comfortable position, but Willow pulled away from the kiss as soon as I did.

"Amelia..." Her fingers went to gently brush the bite marks on my neck. "We probably need to talk about this."

I suppressed a groan, knowing that she was right, but wanting to do anything other than discuss it.

"I'm sorry," Willow said softly, her fingers still tracing the marks. "I saw that Natalie was injured, but... I really thought that she would hold out."

"I wish that were the case, but... The sight Nature gave me still works, even without my wand, and I could see her life-force fading. She didn't want to bite me – she was adamant that she wouldn't – but then she reached the point where... Willow, I think if she'd hesitated even a moment longer, I would have lost her."

Willow sighed. "I know that you didn't have a choice. I just... I feel awful that I prioritised dealing with Dana over making sure that you and Natalie were safe."

"You were on a mission and you had to make a call. And Natalie and I got out of there alive, so there's no reason to get worked up about it."

"You only got out alive because you let Natalie bite you. Because you bonded with her."

I bit my lip. "Are you... Are you mad at me for doing that?"

"What? No. Amelia, Natalie was going to die. I would have done the same thing in your place, but it wouldn't have been as dangerous for me."

I frowned. "Dangerous? There wasn't any danger. Yes, I'm a little light-headed, but I'll recover with rest, and as long as Natalie and I stay separated, the bond will break."

"No, it won't. That's what I meant, Amelia. The bond would have broken if it had been anyone else in that cell with Natalie. But you? The bond only breaks if you and the Vampire *want* it to break."

"Which we both do."

Willow sighed.

"I do want it to break," I protested. "I love you, Willow. I want to bond with *you*, just like we talked about before you were expelled."

"I know, Amelia, and I want that too. But I also know that you love Natalie. Those two things aren't mutually exclusive, and I know that you love me, I don't need it to be at the exclusion of feelings for anyone else, but it does mean that this bond won't break. And that makes it something we'll have to deal with."

I looked away, tears welling in my eyes.

She was right, but I wished she wasn't.

I wished that I could take everything I felt for Natalie and scorch it away.

Natalie clearly had...

And I didn't want to lose Willow over this as well.

I leaned forward, resting my head on Willow's shoulder as she wrapped her arms tight around me, savouring the feel of her as I waited for my feelings to settle enough for me to talk coherently about them.

"It doesn't matter how I feel," I eventually said as I pulled away enough to meet Willow's gaze. "I doubt the bond will hold if Natalie doesn't return those feelings."

"Amelia... You're kidding, right? I think Natalie's been at least a little bit in love with you since that party where you first kissed her."

"Then why was she so fast to jump on breaking the bond?"

"Because she doesn't want to be bonded to someone who is with someone else."

I sighed, looking away as I struggled to accept her words. After all, it just made sense that Natalie wouldn't want to be with me. That Willow wouldn't. Not when I kept failing everyone...

But what she was saying did also make sense. So... Maybe she was right.

"I know," I eventually said. "I know that you're probably right. I just... I know that this complicates things for everyone, and it would be simpler without the bond. And I *want* to be with *you* without complications."

"But her wanting to break the bond still hurts?"

I sighed again. "Are you sure you're not mad at me? Or not even mad, just... You came back to find me bonded to someone else and in the middle of a lot of complicated, messy feelings."

Willow responded by kissing me gently, running her hand gently through my hair as I leaned in closer to her.

I placed my hands on her hips, finding the gap between her shorts and top, my palms settling on soft skin as Willow deepened her kiss.

My heart thundered in my chest as I considered breaking our promise to Freya.

But then irritation started to seep through, causing my muscles to tense.

"Amelia?" Willow asked as she pulled away. "Something wrong?"

"I... I'm not sure..." I frowned as the frustration was replaced by guilt.

But not mine, I realised as I examined it closer.

No, it was Natalie's.

I groaned as I examined her feelings enough to see what had happened.

In the same way I could feel her, she could feel me.

Including everything I had been feeling towards Willow.

Her irritation had then seeped back through the bond, allowing me to feel it.

As soon as she'd realised what had happened, guilt had followed.

"It's the bond," I said sheepishly.

Willow sighed. "Of course. So, Natalie felt... All of that?"

I nodded.

"You can stop your emotions from leaking out if you concentrate, but I think you're too tired to do that right now. Not to mention, I did promise your sister I wouldn't do anything too strenuous with you tonight, and I'm not super eager to get on her bad side, given that I'm pretty sure she could immolate me with a single thought."

I smiled as I laid down and snuggled into her side, choosing to focus on anything but my disappointment at having to rest instead of... Anything else. Especially when I knew Willow was right to insist upon it...

"You sound awfully scared of her for a badass assassin."

Willow frowned a little as she also lay down, turning to face me. "Does it bother you? That I've become a *Fin'hathan?*"

"No. I figured that was probably where you would go. And if I'm not mistaken, you've saved my life twice now. Or was that some other assassin at the listening post outside the school?"

Willow gave me a half shrug. "No, that was me. I was going to drop my glamour, but then Queen Freya showed up and... And I was scared. Especially when you were only hurt so badly because you hesitated, not wanting to hurt the Slayer. I wasn't sure how you would feel about me not showing the same restraint."

"That restraint nearly got me killed."

"I know, but..." Willow sighed. "I know that this work needs to be done. I just wish that it wasn't so damn bloody."

"Then let's work to create a world where the work no longer needs to be done."

Willow smiled, though it didn't quite reach her eyes. "Yeah. Let's do that."

Chapter Two

I groaned as a loud knock awoke me from my sleep, curling up into the figure next to me.

I almost pulled away, worried that Natalie wouldn't want me so close before I remembered that this wasn't Natalie.

No, it was Willow.

And Willow had made it clear last night that she wanted me, no matter what my anxieties tried to claim.

I snuggled further into her, relaxing.

Until another loud knock caused me to groan.

Willow, who was apparently awake, gently stroked my hair before getting up and out of bed.

I just curled up into the warm space she'd left behind.

"Hey," Willow said as she opened the door. "I hope you're not here to get Amelia for classes."

"No," Auntie Jess' familiar voice replied, causing my ears to perk up. "But now that you've had some rest, it seems like a good idea for everyone to talk about what happened yesterday. If you two are feeling up to it, we're going to meet in the infirmary in half an hour."

"I'll let Amelia know."

"Thanks."

At that, the door closed, and Willow made her way back over, climbing back into bed next to me, though she didn't lie down, instead staying upright as she gently stroked my hair.

"So, everyone's meeting in half an hour to talk about what happened."

"I heard."

"Do you want to go?"

I groaned. "No."

"Yeah, me neither. I don't think I can deal with much more of everyone's disappointed face, as if they expected something more of me than becoming *Fin'hathan* after expelling me. But..."

"But?" I asked as I finally sat up to face her.

"But we need to talk to them some time if we want to be involved in whatever the next moves against the Council will be."

I groaned. "Do you really think they'll do anything?"

"I think that they'll need to if they want to avoid the Council putting their people in charge of the Amazons."

I nodded, knowing that she was right, even if I didn't want to do anything other than stay in bed with her all day.

Not when my head was killing me.

Willow sighed as she looked me over. "We should get you something to eat, you're still worn out from yesterday, and you didn't eat last night before falling asleep. Plus, you need to take your medication."

I groaned before practically throwing myself out of the covers, knowing that it was the only way to get myself up. "Yeah, okay, you're right. Just give me five minutes to get dressed."

I grabbed my uniform and changed into my trousers before remembering that I hadn't yet brushed my teeth and was almost completely incapable of brushing my teeth without covering myself in toothpaste.

I headed into the bathroom, still half in my pyjamas, and quickly found my toothbrush.

When I made my way back to the bedroom, Willow was already dressed and had two mugs of coffee and two plates of food.

I smiled as she passed me the one piled high with pastries.

"How did you get dressed and get these so fast?"

Willow raised an eyebrow. "Amelia, you were brushing your teeth for nearly ten minutes."

"Oh," I said before wolfing down one of my pastries. "Sorry. I should have put music on or something to help me focus."

Willow smiled. "You don't have to apologise. We've still got a good fifteen minutes before we're expected anywhere."

I nodded as I finished my food and then found my medication on the bedside table, washing it down with my coffee.

But none of my concentration was on any of that.

No, it was on the way Willow's armour seemed to almost draw light in, keeping it dark. I'd noticed it the day before, but I hadn't had time to really examine the effect.

"So, is that *Fin'hathan* armour?" I asked.

Willow shrugged. "There's not really a uniform, but... My father had it made for me. After everything with the Amazons, he figured it was just a matter of time before I joined him. And he was right. After I was expelled, I called him pretty much immediately." She sighed, placing her hand on the blade at her side and running her thumb over the pommel. "I was sick of watching them keep trying to kill you and being powerless to stop them. I hated that I couldn't stop them from killing Maria or hurting you. That all I could do was get Queen Freya to come to help."

"But that worked," I assured her. "And you did save my life."

Willow gave me a small smile, but it didn't reach her eyes. "I know. But it was too close. What if she hadn't come in time? No, it was too close, and I was too powerless. I'm sick of waiting for other people to save us, Amelia. People who told you it would be safe to go to the Council. That they would play fair. It was so naïve to believe that, and that naïveté almost got you killed. It got me expelled. And yet, it seems everyone telling us not to worry, to let them handle things, is just that naïve. Even Esme... She was so reluctant to take power away from the Amazons who had proven time and time again that they would abuse it, that they were able to see through a plot to kill her. She could have prevented this, and she didn't."

I bit my lip, hating that I knew that she was right, even through the guilt of blaming Esme for not sorting out the Amazons when the consequences had been her death.

And while she had made the initial mistake, maybe if I'd moved faster – done *more* – I could have saved her from it.

And we would still have the one person in a position of authority among Light beings who wasn't just there to retain their own power.

"I don't like the methods the *Fin'hathan* use," Willow said, her voice low as she refused to meet my gaze. "I never have, and I still don't. But... I don't see another way any more. This works, and protecting the people I care about – and the others like me who the Amazons and Council toss aside or worse – matters more to me than giving the Council and their lackeys a second chance."

I made my way over to her and took her hands in mine. "I don't like those methods either, Willow. And I don't think that I could ever use them. But I knew exactly where you would go when you left, and I couldn't blame you. I want to try to find a solution to this that doesn't hurt anyone. But I also don't want to do it at our expense."

"I guess we'll see what the others say and figure out if they have any better solutions. If they have an idea that will actually work, I'll take it, but I am so used to being let down..."

"I know. I am too. But come on. Let's go and see what they have to say."

Willow responded by looking down, and I realised that I was still only half-dressed.

"Just as soon as I find a bra."

———— ⟋⟍ ————

I HURRIED SO MUCH TO finish getting dressed that we ended up arriving at the infirmary early.

When only Natalie was there to greet us.

"Hey," she said, with a slightly awkward wave.

She was moving far more than I was used to, the tension she was feeling clear on her features.

Of course, she still had my blood in her system, topping up her emotional reserves so that her magic was no longer draining all of it.

My hand went to my neck almost subconsciously at the memory.

And then my stomach twisted with guilt.

I frowned. Why was I feeling...

Right. It wasn't me, it was Natalie.

She was feeling guilty that she'd bitten me.

I gave an internal sigh, trying to send back through the bond the thought that she had almost died and biting me under those circumstances wasn't something to feel guilty about.

Any feeling through the bond immediately shut down at that.

The bond was still there. I could still feel it clearly, connecting us through the part of her magic that now lived in me, and the part of mine that lived in her.

But I couldn't feel her emotions as clearly through it.

"Sorry," Natalie said as she tucked a loose strand of long, dark hair behind her ear. "I keep forgetting to close the bond, but I should have done it last night. Especially when... Well, I should have known exactly what would happen when Willow came back."

I shrugged. "It's okay. I would do it myself, but I haven't quite figured it out yet."

"I doubt you would have been able to do it last night. You were so exhausted, and it takes concentration. Really, I should be the one closing it."

"Well, it's closed now," I settled for saying, despite the fact that the closed bond felt strange and almost hollow.

As annoying as it had been, I think I'd preferred it open.

Before either of us could say anything else, the door opened, and Charlotte and Lena came through.

"Hey," I said as they entered, noticing that Lena seemed even more tired than I was. "You okay?"

Lena groaned, rubbing her eyes. "No. I'm still exhausted after holding up the ocean for who knows how long. What about you? I mean, you've got that bond now." She looked between me and Natalie. "Are you two okay?"

"Yeah, I'm fine," I said before I bit my lip as I waited for Natalie to respond, wondering just what exactly she would say about her feelings on the bond.

But before she could, Charlotte folded her arms. "To be honest, in your shoes, I would be less worried about the bond and more worried about... Well, what happened to Esme. Are you okay after that?"

I shrugged again. "I just... I just wish that I could have acted quicker. That I could have done something."

"Me too," Natalie said. "I moved as fast as I could, but..."

"It wasn't your fault."

We all turned at the sound of Sarah's voice as she entered the room, along with Freya, Auntie Jess and Ms Griffin.

If Lena and I looked tired, Sarah looked exhausted, and I suspected she hadn't slept all night.

"Really, girls," she continued, "don't blame yourselves. We never should have trusted information that came from one of Dana's people. We never should have trusted Dana's people at all. We should have kicked them out of any position of power as soon as Esme took over, and damn what anyone said about it proving that we refused to listen to our critics."

I frowned. "Was that what the other Amazons said about Esme?"

"Of course, it was. As soon as she won the election, we were putting out fires. All of Dana's people were suddenly very loudly concerned that we would become authoritarian despots who wouldn't listen to criticism. Esme was so worried about proving them right that she tried to bring them into the fold. And we all saw how well that went..."

"It seems like you were counselling her against it."

"I was, but I'm still young for a Witch, Amelia. Esme took me seriously because she was capable of seeing past that. But the other Witches aren't. It's why there isn't a suitable replacement for Esme. Esme never played by Dana's rules, but most like her don't survive magical politics. The only ones that do are the ones who play along, and none of them will inspire the same respect as Esme. The only ones who kept to her example are too young to have burned out. And therefore, too young to replace her."

Freya frowned. "Are you sure that you can't replace her, Sarah? You were her second-in-command, and the young Witches won't care about your age."

Sarah shook her head. "Even if that were true... My husband is a Master Slayer, Freya. *I* know that he's a good person, but a lot of Esme's supporters won't risk letting Slayers close to the Amazons. They're going through the same disconnect as the Amazons over whether or not to support the Council, but they don't have an equivalent to Esme to rally defiance. Chris is trying, but... Well, his youth works in his favour, as he's one of the youngest Slayers to ever become a Master, but that's still balanced against the fact that the older Slayers have had a lot longer to fight together and earn each other's trust. If he can rally them, and if they show enough of a change to satisfy Esme's supporters, it might work. But I suspect that the only thing big enough would be a permanent break with the Council."

Willow stepped forward. "You've got time as Esme's successor before they force an election, though."

Sarah nodded. "Yes, they'll give me a few weeks while people mourn, but I don't have much power to do anything other than keep things running in place."

"We don't need anything too drastic. At least, not in public. But there's no point in discussing a successor until you've made sure to get all of Dana's spies from your circle. Otherwise, they'll plant one of their own as Esme's successor in this next election, or sabotage anyone you choose from the inside."

"You're right, and I have some idea of where to start."

"You need to be thorough. When the *Fin'hathan* and I investigated the situation... Well, there were signs that some Witches loyal to Dana might have kept under the radar. You need to catch them as well."

Sarah frowned a little in thought, taking a moment to measure her options. "I was thinking through the night... Anyone involved in running Themiscyra used to have to swear that nothing came before their work and duty to the Amazons. Including the pursuit of their own power. Of course, while it was meant to prevent corruption, many thought it discriminated against Witches with families, so the practice was disbanded. But... Esme did always like it. She suggested an amendment that wouldn't include families in the oath, but it never went anywhere. Still, if I ask people to say the oath at her funeral, it will prove who is actually loyal to Themiscyra. Though there would need to be some adjustment so that everyone could take the oath at once. Maybe using the focus crystals planted around Themiscyra..."

I cringed. "Are you sure you want to use her funeral for a political move?"

I felt bad as long as the words left my mouth. I hadn't meant to sound so judgemental, I was just worried that this might not be something Sarah could deal with in the long-term.

"I'm sure that it's what Esme would want," Sarah eventually said.

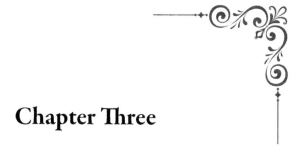

Chapter Three

M s Griffin suggested that I take a few days to recover from everything, rather than returning to classes.

That was mostly fine with me, as Maria's memories gave me a head-start on classes anyway.

But it did lead to me just sitting around my and Willow's room with nothing to do.

"Bored?" Willow asked as I kept producing orbs of coloured light from my wand, until they nearly overtook the room.

The wand still didn't feel right. I'd gone back to the old second-hand one I'd used to use, but it wasn't the same, my magic refusing to flow through it as easily as the wand I'd lost.

I sighed. "Kind of." I waved my wand, causing the orbs to disappear. I didn't want to admit that it wasn't just boredom eating away at me. No, I kept *seeing* it. Esme collapsing and Natalie almost dying and Maria...

Without something to distract me, it's all I could think about.

I should have been better. I should have been able to save them, and everyone would figure that out eventually and give up on me.

Willow and Freya and even Auntie Jess... They just couldn't see that this was my fault, and when they did...

Whenever this happened, I usually did whatever I could to prove myself. To make up for my mistakes by becoming better.

No, not just better. By becoming the best.

But now I had a sub-par wand and nothing to do except sit back and wait for Sarah to make the next move.

I put my wand away. "Maybe I'll go and see if Freya has any more information on anything that's happened. Want to come with me?"

Willow bit her lip, twisting her hands around each other for a moment before asking, "Do you think she'll mind?"

"Why would she mind?"

"Well... She trusts you because you're her sister, but I'm..."

"Her sister's girlfriend. And you were the one to save us on that last mission, so if you did need to prove yourself, that would have more than done it."

"Right... Okay..."

I gave her a reassuring smile as I stood up. "Is this because she's the Queen of the Underworld?"

"Of course, it is. And she's also a Daughter of Nature."

"You've met Nature herself. And she was encouraging us to... Well, you know... So, I don't know how you can be nervous."

Willow sighed, folding her arms. "Well, that was so surreal, I didn't really have time to be nervous. But with Freya... What if she doesn't like me? What if she doesn't think I'm good enough for her sister?"

"Why wouldn't she like you? You're great."

"I'm an assassin."

I shrugged. "Didn't Freya used to work as a bounty hunter before she realised that she was the heir to the throne?"

"Well... I guess..."

"So, she's got no room to talk. Now, come on. Let's go and see if she's got any new leads."

Willow nodded, relaxing a little, but not entirely.

No, I suspected that wouldn't happen until we were talking with Freya and Willow realised that she had nothing to worry about.

We headed out into the corridor and down to Freya's room.

I knocked on the door, hearing "Come in," in response.

I opened the door and Willow hesitated, staying behind me, as I entered.

"Hey, Amy," Freya said with a smile from the small sofa in the corner as I entered and realised that her hair was tied up with various, multi-coloured accessories.

Then I saw Princess Katherine sitting next to her, a pink brush in her hand.

"Hey," I said as I stepped through and Freya peered out.

"Hey Willow," she said, and Willow jumped at her words. "You can come in."

Willow's cheeks quickly turned red as she stepped into the room. "I... Of course, Your Majesty."

Freya rolled her eyes. "Nope, you're not allowed to call me by any titles as long as you're dating my sister. It's too weird. Please, just call me Freya."

"I... Of course, Freya."

Princess Katherine then immediately bounded forward, leaving her brush stuck firmly in her mother's hair. "Auntie Amy! Is this your girlfriend?"

I smiled. "Yes, she is."

Katherine then turned to Willow, looking over her armour with wide eyes. "Wow... When I'm older, I want a girlfriend just as pretty as you."

I couldn't help but smile, my heart melting a little at the fact that Katherine felt so comfortable saying that when she was so young.

But I supposed that was to be expected when both of her parents were bi.

Willow hesitated for a moment before smiling back at her. "I'm sure that you'll find one."

Freya shook her head as she removed the brush from her hair before standing up and making her way over. "Kath, weren't you just saying yesterday that you wanted a pretty boyfriend?"

"I can have both! You do!"

Freya smiled. "Yeah, I guess that's true. And speaking of my pretty husband, why don't you go and find your dad? I think he's with Gail in her office."

"Okay!"

Katherine then raced out of the room.

Freya sighed as she turned to us. "She's getting restless with me and Damon away from home. But hopefully if Sarah gets the Amazons out from under the Council's control, they'll lose their grip on Witches, and that will mean that they can no longer threaten to boycott the school. Which means that we can go home."

My stomach twisted at the thought of Freya leaving, but if we won this fight, then she really wouldn't have to stay.

"So," Freya said, turning her attention to me, "did you pop by because you needed something?"

"No, not really. I just wanted to see if you had any more information on what the Council are up to."

Freya sighed. "Unfortunately not. They seem to have gone quiet, which I am not taking as a good sign. But until they rear their heads again, there's not really anything we can do aside from wait to see if Sarah's plan at the funeral works."

Freya then looked me over. "But if you're bored and looking for something to do, why don't I try training you and Willow together? Assuming you're both up for it, training together will give you an advantage when you do return to the fight."

I turned to Willow, almost bouncing on the spot. If Freya trained me... Well, maybe I could prove that I wasn't such a failure after all. "What do you think? Are you up for some training?"

Willow nodded. "Of course. I can't imagine a better way to hone my powers than training under a Daughter of Nature."

"Well then," Freya said, "let's head to the woods and find a spacious clearing. This isn't something we want to do either inside or near prying eyes."

I nodded, following her out of the room, with Willow following close behind.

Freya turned to Willow as we walked. "Though, you should probably temper your expectations a bit. As much as I'm a Daughter of Nature, I was pretty much entirely self-taught. I didn't have long with the one real teacher I had for my elemental abilities, though she did teach me to appreciate air as an element. And that letting go was never a strength of mine..."

Her gaze dropped to the ground at that as a slight breeze moved through her hair, still decorated with various plastic clips.

I frowned as I remembered Aaron saying something about Freya falling for her Elven teacher.

"What happened to her?" I asked, and Freya shrugged.

"Politics," she said, and I thought she might leave it at that before she sighed after several moments and elaborated. "Lord Uther blackmailed her into working against me by kidnapping her parents. I managed to free them, and Isabelle was going to work with me to bring Uther's crimes to light. But then Uther had her poisoned, and there's no known cure. I've been slowly healing her with my magic, but it's been years, and I suspect it will be several more before it will be safe from her to wake."

Willow frowned. "You've been healing her for so long? Isn't that a drain on your magic?"

"Well, yes. But... I couldn't imagine just leaving her." Freya shrugged. "Maybe I wouldn't have done it for someone I wasn't falling in love with, but the idea of leaving anyone to die like that... I just couldn't do it."

"So, you two were together?"

Freya nodded. "And Damon. Though I don't think he ever got over finding out that she was working for Uther, even if he had been blackmailing her."

"So, what are you going to do when she wakes up? I mean, you already have the two marriages allowed by Demon law."

Freya sighed. "You know, I hate arbitrary rules more than almost anything, and this whole limit on bonding is as arbitrary as it gets. I grew up being told that I could only have one partner, and then I found out that by Demon laws I could have two. But if it could be two, why not more?" She shook her head. "It's not something I need to worry about right now, but it is frustrating.

"And it's not something Isabelle will be bothered by. She was quite clear when we started dating that Elves don't usually stick to just one or two partners."

Willow shrugged. "They didn't, back in Skyreach – before it was cut off from Earth – but those of us who never knew a home there don't always have the same attitudes. I mostly grew up with my mother at a coven, so I only really know these things through my dad's stories, though I suppose I can understand the appeal."

I bit my lip at her words, trying not to think back to the discussions Natalie and I had had before she'd come back.

About how her opinion on the matter was really the only thing keeping us from giving in to our feelings for each other.

My hand went to the bite marks on my neck, reminding me that things had gotten far more complicated.

And Natalie had clearly changed her mind about all of that, wanting to sever the bond between us.

Freya turned back to Willow as we passed through the first of the trees that made up the woods outside the school. "How did your mother react to you becoming *Fin'hathan* if she's a Witch?"

Willow shrugged awkwardly, not meeting Freya's gaze. "I guess I haven't really told her... I rang my dad pretty much as soon as I was expelled, so I never went home. I think he told her, but I've got no idea what her reaction was. She probably just told my father to keep me away from the coven. They were never happy with my father's line of work, and they never really accepted me, always afraid I was going to join him. I don't want to cause trouble for my mother by proving them right."

Freya frowned. "If the coven never accepted you, why didn't your mother move?"

"She didn't think it would be better anywhere else, and I can't blame her for that. Most covens are pretty insular and distrustful of outsiders. Though, as I got older and learned more about the Guardians, I did start to wonder why we couldn't move to the city. But I know that my mum isn't the type to risk leaving the coven system for something so unknown."

"She should have if it might have been a better place for you."

"It's fine," Willow said with another small shrug. "I understand why she would stick with what was familiar instead of risking the change. And after Ember Academy opened, it gave me a place to go anyway." She then straightened her posture, a determined look replacing her previously unsure expression. "Not to mention, if we can break the hold of the Council and their ideas on the covens, it should mean that no one like me had to go through that again."

We made it to a new clearing in the woods, for which I was glad, realising that as we had been walking, I had been tensing.

Readying myself to return to the spot where we had buried Maria.

But of course, Freya wouldn't take me there.

No, she'd found somewhere new for us to train.

As we arrived, Damon shifted in next to Freya, Katherine on his back.

Freya smiled as she saw them. "All done with Gail?"

"Yes," Damon said. "And Kath mentioned that Amy had stopped by. I figured that meant that you would go for training, and I thought that I might help."

"Well, I can't deny that some help might be nice." Freya then turned to me and Willow, looking us over for a moment.

"Actually, I think you two might benefit from learning how Damon and I work together. Amy, Damon tells me that you have a preference for using Dark Energy, just like he does, and Willow, you can obviously control air like me. So, why don't we try teaching you how to use your powers in the same ways we do, and then we can do some test fights against each other. Though, Amy, we should probably also focus on the powers Nature gave you."

I nodded, glad to finally be doing something other than waiting around.

"OW..." I GROANED AS I dropped to the ground for what felt like the dozenth time.

"Sorry," Freya said as I turned to see that Willow was similarly defeated, though she was already on her way back up to her feet. "Maybe we're going too hard on you."

I frowned as I got back to my feet. "You've said that the last ten times you've beaten us. At this point, you couldn't be going any easier."

Freya sighed. "It's just the difference in experience, Amy. And the fact that I'm an Angel, and you're using a wand that you're not really attached to, won't be helping."

Willow shook her head. "No, it's not just that. I know how to fight more powerful opponents, and even with a wand she's not attached to, Amy's still more powerful than most Witches. No, the problem is that you and Prince Damon are bonded. That bond allows you to know where you both are at any given time, and how you're each going to move. That's what's giving you the advantage."

My stomach twisted as I remembered that Willow and I had once intended to bond.

Back before she'd been expelled.

In fact, the only reason we hadn't was that she'd been expelled before we could.

And now...

Willow sighed, shaking her head. "Amelia should be training with Natalie, not me."

Freya brushed a stray strand of hair from her eyes before placing her hands on her hips. "She should be training with anyone she might fight alongside. But that can't be Natalie right now. They need to stay away from each other if they hope to ever break the bond between them, and combat training isn't staying away."

Willow rolled her eyes. "Except the bond isn't going to break, and we all know it."

Freya just sighed, not arguing with Willow's assertion. "Perhaps it won't," she eventually said. "But it's worth a try. Especially when Natalie has made it clear that she wants to break it." She finally turned to me, rather than just talking about me. "You and Natalie are still young, Amy, and bonding isn't something to rush into."

Willow spoke up before I could. "But sometimes not rushing into things means going against our nature, and that's not always a positive. I mean, all the stories say that you and Prince Damon knew each other from being teenagers, and the only thing that kept you apart was not knowing that the other had magic. If you had known the truth when you were younger, would you have hesitated to bond?"

Freya and Damon both exchanged a look that said that they very much wouldn't have.

Freya turned back to Willow with a sigh. "We might not have, but that's because we both would have *wanted* to bond. But as I said, Natalie has made it more than clear-"

"All right," I said, cutting her off. I couldn't take any more of being told exactly how much Natalie didn't want to bond with me. "I think we get it. Natalie doesn't want to bond, so I shouldn't train with her. I'm fine with that, so can you both just leave it be. Please."

Thankfully, both Freya and Willow nodded.

"Okay," Freya said. "I think we settled the matter. I would say that we should return to training now, but it's getting on and I think we could all use some lunch. We can meet back up this afternoon, or if you'd rather, you can take a break for the rest of today. You never want to overdo training."

I turned to Willow, who just shrugged.

"I guess we'll see how we feel after lunch," I settled for saying.

WE GOT SOME FOOD BEFORE classes let out for lunch and brought it back to our room, not wanting to risk running into Natalie.

Not when distance was needed to break the bond.

I sensed within my magic as Willow and I settled down to eat, finding the tie to Natalie more than easily.

It didn't feel like it had gotten any weaker.

No, I could still feel her clearly, realising that she was heading out of class to get some food, a ravenous hunger clawing at her throat.

But not for food, I realised as she clamped down on the feeling.

No, she was craving blood.

My blood, specifically.

And she was doing everything in her power to try to ignore that fact.

I stopped examining the bond so closely, not wanting to spy on Natalie. I really had just meant to see how strong the bond was.

But now I couldn't quite shake the distant feel of her hunger.

And the memory of how good it would feel to sate it.

I did my best to ignore that thought, focusing on my girlfriend.

And the way she was frowning at her food.

She hadn't really been all that talkative since we'd finished training.

Since she'd realised that the thing holding us back from fighting with Freya and Damon on equal footing was that Freya and Damon were bonded, and we weren't.

"Willow," I eventually said, my voice barely coming out as more than a whisper. I might have been sure that we needed to talk about this, but that didn't mean that I wanted to. Not when there were too many terrifying places the conversation could go... "Do you regret that we never bonded?"

She looked up in surprise, clearly not having expected that question. But after a moment to consider my words, she sighed. "Of course, I do, Amelia. When we were separated... Being separated from your bonded isn't fun, but it would have at least been *something*. *Fin'hathan* are so careful about communications when you're at their base or on missions for them... I just wanted some way to communicate with you. To know that you were okay. To be there for you after Maria..."

I winced at the reminder and Willow sighed.

"I'm sorry, I didn't mean to bring it up. I just... I wanted to be there for you."

"I wanted to be there for you as well," I said, my voice barely coming out as more than a whisper as I put everything I had into stopping tears from falling at the reminder of everything that had happened when she'd left. "The Council screwed you over, and I wanted to be there for you. And if we had been connected through a bond, I could have been. And then..."

She sighed. "And then you could have told me how badly Natalie was hurt through the bond, and you wouldn't have had to let her bite you."

I bit my lip. "Are you sure you're not upset about that?"

She nodded. "I'm sure, Amelia. She would have died otherwise, and I was the one who decided not to focus on freeing you."

I decided to refocus, not wanting to turn a conversation about us into a conversation about Natalie.

Even if it was difficult to avoid.

"But if we ignore the convenience," I continued, "would you still regret not having bonded? If we weren't factoring in that it would let us communicate across distances, I mean."

Willow responded by reaching out, taking my hand in hers. I lifted my gaze up to meet hers, seeing that she was resolute as she said, "Of course. I love you, Amelia. I want to be your bonded more than anything."

"Then why don't we bond now?" I asked, my mouth running away with the errant thought before I even realised what I was saying. But then the words were out of my mouth and... Well, I did want this, so what would be the point of taking them back? "I mean, Demons can have two magical bonds, right? So, it must be possible."

Willow sighed, tucking a loose strand of hair behind her ear. "It is, and I do want to bond with you, but... Amelia, I don't want this to be something that we do just because everything is confusing with Natalie right now. Or something that we do just to make our fighting better. I want it to be because *we* want to be together, and for no other reason."

"It wouldn't be-"

Willow silenced me with a look, her sharp gaze telling me that she wasn't going to believe any argument I had.

Which was probably fair. As much as I had wanted this before...

Well, could I honestly say that I was doing this for the purest of reasons?

Willow then sighed. "Look, even if everything else were perfect, we shouldn't do this right now. Your bond with Natalie is still new, and the two of us bonding now might mess with it. It might stop you from breaking the bond or change the bond in ways we can't imagine. It's not worth the risk."

I nodded, knowing that she was probably right.

But none of that erased the sting of knowing that she no longer wanted to bond with me.

Willow didn't want me, Natalie didn't want me...

I should have known that thinking that they would was ridiculous. When had anyone ever wanted me? Even my parents didn't have time for me.

I'd thought that coming to Ember Academy, and realising that I liked girls and not boys, had fixed everything.

But it hadn't, had it?

I was still just as broken as ever, and I still kept letting everyone down.

I'd let down Maria, I'd let down Esme, and now I was letting down both Natalie and Willow by being too caught in the middle for either of them to want.

I tried to just focus on my lunch, but I struggled to find my appetite as one nagging question just wouldn't leave; who would I let down next?

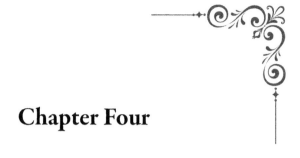

Chapter Four

Willow and I spent the next few days training with Freya, heading out to the clearing in the woods early in the morning, taking a short break, and only heading back once we were thoroughly exhausted.

"Amelia," Willow said, drawing my attention as I put my armour on several days into training.

"Yeah?" I answered as I finished with the clasps.

"Why don't we only train in the morning today, and take a break this afternoon?"

I frowned. "Take a break? Why? We're making good progress."

"We are, but we're training right up until you're two seconds away from passing out. I just... I don't feel like we're spending any time together outside of training. Which is time we're also spending with your sister."

I frowned. "I need this training, Willow. In case you haven't noticed, I'm still several steps behind you. If I intend to catch up before the Council makes their next move-"

Willow cut me off by moving over to me and tracing her fingertips over my left arm.

Right where my scars were.

"One afternoon off isn't going to kill you, Amelia. And you need it. The last time you pushed yourself this hard, you almost died."

I looked away, my throat tightening.

Willow had never referred to that night as a failure before.

I'd thought of it as one, but she'd always countered that I had saved her life by taking the curse into myself.

There had always been the persistent voice in the back of my head, telling me that she wouldn't have needed saving if I hadn't screwed up in the first place.

I'd always been able to push it away with the knowledge that that wasn't how Willow saw things.

But... What if it was how she saw things now?

Did she blame me for dragging her into danger that I didn't understand, and then having to almost kill myself to get her out of it again?

How could she not? I'd always been shocked that she hadn't seen it earlier. It only made sense that she saw it now.

I pulled away from her touch. "That was before I knew what I was doing. I'm not new to magic any more. I know how far I can push myself. And I also know that I need to push myself as far as possible if I hope to take down the Council."

Willow sighed before nodding. "All right. I guess we should head down to the clearing then."

"I guess we should," I said before storming off down the corridor and out of the building.

Freya smiled in greeting as we arrived in the clearing. "Good morning, girls. Ready for another day of training?"

Willow answered before I could. "Actually, I was thinking that we should just train this morning, and then take a break this afternoon. We've been working at a pretty break-neck pace and Amelia could probably do with a few hours when she's not training or sleeping."

I glared at Willow, not believing that she was dragging Freya into this.

And especially not that she was dragging her into this by suggesting that I couldn't handle our current training routine.

Freya looked me up and down for a moment before nodding. "You know, I think Willow's right, Amy. A little rest would be good for you."

I turned my glare to Freya. Did everyone here think that I was incapable of setting my own training schedule? That I was a child who needed her hand held through all of this?

"I'm fine," I growled. "And I don't need to be patronised. If I was struggling, I would tell you, but I'm not. I am more than capable of handling this training routine."

Dark Energy crackled under my skin as I struggled to draw breath.

It was clear from the way that Freya was looking at me that she didn't believe me.

She didn't and Willow didn't, and of course they didn't.

Why would I expect anyone to see me as capable and competent when I wasn't? When I was just a stupid child who was going to get everyone killed.

Freya hesitated for a moment before reaching out to me.

The move shocked me, and the Dark Energy I was barely containing beneath my skin blasted forth without prompt.

Freya stumbled back.

My breath refused to come in anything but short, sharp bursts.

Shit.

I was worried that they saw me as a child, but now? Now they would definitely think that I was just throwing a tantrum.

And, wasn't I? Shouldn't I be better than this? Better than this black hole of fury and pain consuming me from the inside out?

Why couldn't I stop feeling like this?

My legs were moving before I could think better of it, getting me away from the clearing – away from Freya and Willow – before I could do anything else to hurt them.

And before they could voice the things I was already thinking.

That I had screwed up.

That I couldn't stop screwing up.

That they were giving up on me, just like everyone else...

I had no idea where I was running to, but then I stepped through some dense trees, and stepped out in Nature's clearing.

Nature was standing there, waiting for me, in her wolf form.

I just stared at her, unable to truly relax.

Why had she brought me here? Was it to give Freya the chance to catch up with me.

Nature responded by moving over to me, rubbing her nose against my hand.

I moved my hand up to her ears and stroked gently.

I found myself relaxing a little, certain that Nature had brought me here because she knew that I had to get away, not because she was waiting for Freya to find me.

I sighed as my throat tightened, struggling to stop the tears welling in my eyes from falling.

"I'm such an idiot," I muttered. "Creator, I just shouldn't be around people, should I? Why did I get so upset? It was like... I just couldn't stop imagining the worst. And now I've lashed out and everyone probably hates me for it. Or thinks I'm some immature child who can't handle her emotions..."

I kept stroking Nature's fur for several more moments before asking, "Can I just stay here with you forever? Instead of going back, I mean."

Nature huffed before removing her head from my hand and heading to the other end of the clearing, and the part of her magic that resided within me insisted that she wanted me to follow.

"Hey, wait," I said as I chased after her, wondering where exactly she was heading.

Nature passed through the trees, out of the clearing, and I followed, stopping as I realised that the clearing had let us out in front of a large stone wall.

A large wall that was slightly curved, with a wooden door in the middle.

Maria's memories sang within me as I realised where we were.

"Maria's tower," I said aloud as I reached my hand out to the doorknob, the feel far too familiar.

I'd never come in this way. I'd always just... appeared.

But gripping the doorknob still somehow felt like coming home.

I opened the door to reveal a large stone staircase.

I hesitated for just a moment before making my way to the stairs, Nature following alongside.

I was grateful for her presence, my fingers instinctively reaching out to brush her fur as we slowly made our way up the large stone steps.

Slowly making our way to the top.

I wasn't sure what I expected when we got there, but when I took the final few steps and saw that everything was exactly how Maria left it, I was somehow surprised.

As if the tower should have known that she was gone and... And done *something*.

Packed her things away out of respect, maybe.

But no, there was no one here to do that.

Maria and I were the only ones who'd known about the tower, and I hadn't come back here since she'd died.

I slowly moved through the space, refamiliarising myself with everything.

I knew that I had only been a projection when I'd come here in the past, but it wasn't until I was moving through the space now that I realised just how tenuous my connection to the space had been before.

Everything now lacked the dreamlike quality I'd gotten used to. It felt real. Tangible.

Because it was, I supposed.

I paused as I moved through to the small kitchenette. The extent of food-prep area that Maria had needed, along with a small table and a single chair.

I hadn't been able to eat while I was there, after all.

And I had been the only one who ever visited.

The only one in this time who knew that this place existed.

Well, except for Nature, but she was practically a god, so I didn't think her knowledge counted.

I had been the only one Maria had trusted with this location.

And even that hadn't really been trust.

No, our magic had just latched onto each other's after enough exposure.

Like it knew that we were both drowning and needed each other.

And now she was gone.

And the only person who knew about this place now was me.

Maria's secret hideout.

Was that why Nature had brought me here? Because I'd asked to escape the pain of trying and failing over and over and over again?

I couldn't let anyone down if I never inflicted myself upon anyone.

The room started to flicker around me.

Just as it had when I'd relived Maria's memories.

But that had been because the bond had been unstable. And the bond was gone now...

But the room didn't seem to care, reshaping into an older, much messier version.

With Maria standing by her stock of potions, swiftly rifling through them.

Her movements were choppy and erratic, and her eyes were red and puffy.

She'd been crying.

"Don't do this, Maria."

I turned to the voice at the door, seeing a figure I'd seen once before in Maria's memories.

The second Queen of the Underworld, and the sister of Maria's beloved, Helena.

Maria spun on her heel to face the Queen before grabbing her wand in one hand and a dark vial in the other.

She threw the vial at the Queen's feet, but she stepped through the ensuing smoke without it affecting her.

She moved faster than Maria, her heavily armoured hand gripping Maria in place.

"I am the Queen of all Demons," she said as Maria struggled, but could not move. "Did you really think Nightmare was going to affect me?"

Maria glared at her. "It would have if you had a heart. You killed your sister. That should have left more than enough scars for the Nightmare to seep into."

"I did what I had to."

"What you had to? You took our future from us. You forced me to break up with her, and when she... When she got angry and upset, you killed her for it. You told me that breaking up with her would save her and I... I was stupid enough to believe you."

The Queen sighed, her conviction fading, but she didn't let Maria go. "You know that you can't kill me. We both know that. The only way this revenge quest of yours ends is with you dead. And I think that's the point.

"Don't destroy yourself over this, Maria. The world already lost one brilliant woman in this mess. Don't make it two."

The Queen then shifted out, leaving Maria to slump forward alone.

More tears fell down Maria's face and her shoulders moved in silent sobs.

She dragged herself over to the alcove in the corner, where there was a bed just big enough for two.

Another difference from my time, where it was only big enough for Maria.

On the bed were several books, written in intricately looping handwriting that I couldn't make heads nor tails of.

But Maria picked up one of the books and the knowledge and memories she'd left to me told me what they were.

Helena's notes.

And the passage Maria's fingers kept brushing over and over were the notes Helena had made on ways for the two of them to use magic to have a child together.

Plans that she hadn't told Maria about. Plans she had decided to keep to herself until she could make sure that they were both powerful enough to be left alone.

But her sister had grown worried before that point, thinking that Helena intended to fight her for the throne.

So, she'd told Maria to break up with her, thinking that it was her influence making her worse.

Her miscalculation was in not realising that Maria had been holding her back.

And with nothing ahead of her and nothing else to lose, Helena had become the very threat her sister had feared.

And it had ended in her death.

"I'm sorry," Maria muttered to the book, repeating the words over and over and over again.

I knew that she couldn't hear or see me – that I wasn't even really there – but I moved to sit next to her anyway.

"I know that you blame yourself for Helena's death. That you think that if you hadn't listened to her sister, she would still be alive. And maybe she would be. But that doesn't make you responsible. Helena and her sister made their own choices after you broke up. They're the ones who did this.

"And, you know, there are people who need you. You haven't met them yet, but you will. And you'll form your own coven, giving a home to people who need it. It doesn't erase this mistake, but... It gets better. You keep going and you keep trying, and it gets better. And that never happens if you give in to the despair of your mistakes. Even if it sometimes seems like Litcorde and Sisters like us only ever make mistakes..."

At that, Maria disappeared.

And I was left with just Nature.

I turned to her, tears in my eyes.

"I have to go back, don't I? I have to keep going?"

Nature rubbed her head against my hand, and I took that as a 'yes'.

"It's so exhausting," I admitted. "Having to pick myself up time after time after time."

I sighed as I stroked Nature's fur. "But Maria managed it. And if I could be kind to her... Maybe I could extend that to myself as well."

I shook my head. "You know, it would be nice if maybe once in a while it was someone else being kind to me. Realising that I needed someone else to say that I'm not a fuck-up. That I'll be okay. But... I guess if I'm all I've got, then I'll have to make do."

My tears finally fell at that point, exhaustion washing over me as I realised that I had brought form to Maria's memories.

Casting a spell without intending to.

And without a wand I was properly attuned to.

I passed out on Maria's bed.

Chapter Five

I groaned as I awoke, realising that I had gone to sleep.

I took my phone from my pocket and sighed.

I'd slept through the night.

Which, given the exhaustion that still permeated me, made sense.

Casting a spell that powerful without a real wand was dangerous.

I was lucky I just passed out...

My stomach rumbled, telling me that I should probably head back, but I couldn't quite bring myself to leave.

I headed back through the room, my gaze drawn to a long wooden box on Maria's desk.

Her knowledge told me that it was a finding system. She would magically bond an object to it, and if she ever lost the object, it would appear back in the box.

I headed over to it, my curiosity guiding me as I opened the box.

And found Maria's wand.

Of course, she would use the finding system for her wand. I should probably do the same.

If I still had a wand that I was attuned to.

I sighed as I reached down, my fingers gently brushing Maria's wand as I realised that it would likely never be used again.

A girl without a wand and a wand without an owner.

What a pair we were...

But as soon as my fingers touched the wood of her wand, I felt something from it.

The stirrings of magic.

Asking for permission.

I frowned, reaching my own magic out in response, trying to get a better sense of why the wand was waking.

And what it was responding to.

As it awoke further, I realised that it was responding to what remained of Maria's magic within me.

And asking me to bond with it.

I frowned. Would that even work? Second-hand wands never attuned as well as wands you found yourself.

But then, this had been Maria's wand, and it was already responding to her magic within me.

I reached out with the rest of my magic, allowing the wand to bond with me.

My magic immediately came into focus.

Just like it had with the wand Nature had given me.

It attuned to me just as easily as if I'd found it myself.

As if it belonged to me.

I sighed a breath of relief, my magic finally in focus.

Finally in my control.

I put it in my pocket before heading back down the stairs.

It was time to return to the real world.

As I left the tower and walked through the trees, I arrived in Nature's clearing once more.

Only I wasn't alone.

Willow sat on one of the boulders, scrolling through her phone.

As soon as I stepped into the clearing, she looked up, and smiled.

"Willow?" I asked as I approached. "How did you get here?"

"Freya brought me. She knew that you were with Nature, and she thought that Nature would bring you here. But then we got here and no one was around... Well, I thought it would be the best place to wait for you. Wherever Nature took you, I figured you would return here."

"How long have you been waiting?"

She shrugged sheepishly. "All night."

I cringed. "Willow, I am so sorry, I had no idea. I didn't mean to pass out, I swear, I just-"

"It's okay," Willow said. "I didn't mind spending the night out here. It's quiet here, and I like being able to sleep somewhere under the stars, where I know it's safe."

"Still. I'm sorry. For... Everything."

Willow smiled. "It's okay, Amelia. Really. Are you okay? You seemed upset yesterday."

I sighed as I made my way over to her, not wanting to talk across the clearing. "I'm better. I'm sorry... I want to explain, but... I'm not even sure where to start."

She extended her hand, Energy crackling over it. "Well, we could just start here."

I stared at her hand, taking a moment to realise what she meant.

When we'd trained with Energy, it had allowed us to share what we were feeling.

I bit my lip. "Willow... I *am* feeling better, but better doesn't mean a hell of a lot here. I don't want to subject you to this."

"Amelia, I'm your girlfriend. You're my Ni'tal. I'm here for you. No matter how bad this is."

I nodded, still getting the sense that I didn't know the real meaning behind that Elven word she used for me.

My throat tightened as I reached out and took her hand.

Everything flowed through my Energy.

My grief and guilt over losing Maria and then Esme, and the omnipresent feeling that I could have done something different.

I could have saved them.

But I didn't, and now Natalie didn't want anything to do with me, Willow didn't want to bond with me, and after I lashed out at her, Freya would probably never want to see me again.

I was losing everyone, and I didn't know how to stop it.

How to plug the hole of despair eating me from the inside out.

And poisoning everyone around me.

Tears welled in Willow's eyes and I pulled away, realising that I'd done the exact thing I'd been afraid of.

I'd hurt her.

"I'm sorry," I managed, but Willow shook her head.

"No, Amelia, don't. You don't have to apologise. I told you I could handle it and I could." She wiped away her tears. "I'm not upset because you hurt me. I'm upset because I care about you. Because that was... Years and years of feeling like you were never enough all just bubbling away under the surface until you couldn't ignore them any more."

I looked away, hating that she was right. Hating that she had pinpointed the issue so quickly.

"Coming to Ember Academy was supposed to be a fresh start," I eventually said, barely keeping my voice from cracking. "Where I could finally not be remembered as a fuck-up. I was a Witch, and Maria even said that I was a *good* one. And I figured out that I liked girls so, you know, that solved my dating problems. And... And I just thought that everything would be okay. That I could have a fresh start. Where I could prove that I wasn't worthless..."

Willow then moved her hand to my shoulder, gently tracing my armour, where my scars were beneath. "Amelia... You try *so hard* to prove yourself. To the point of nearly killing yourself, over and over again. And I'm willing to bet that's exactly how you ended up on the path to Oxford or Cambridge.

"I'm not asking you to slow down because I think you can't handle it, I'm asking because I know that you can, but I also know the cost. And I love you too much to lose you, Amelia. Just the thought of it kills me."

She closed the space between us, kissing me slow and deep, as her Energy crackled, reinforcing her words as it allowed me to feel her concern for me.

And how it came from love.

She pulled away after a moment, though not too far, her forehead resting gently against mine.

"And just for the record, I do want to bond with you. I want nothing more than to bond with you right this second, my Ni'tal. But while I wasn't sure exactly what was bothering you, I could sense that *something* was going on. It didn't seem like the right time for you to make permanent decisions like this."

"Except it's not a decision I'm making now. It's a decision I made before you left."

"I know, and trust me, I'm struggling to hold off on bonding with you right now. But I really think that you need to sort things out with Natalie first. That's nothing to do with how I feel about you, it's just... Me trying to be sensible."

I sighed. "As much as I wish that you weren't right, I know that you are. But I swear, the second we have things sorted with Natalie..."

Willow smiled before kissing me once more.

My hands went to her waist, keeping her close as I returned her kiss with everything I had.

Eventually, she pulled away. "How about we have a lazy morning?" she asked. "I also wanted to slow down so that we could actually spend some time together. It's been forever since we've just *talked*."

"You know, I think I'd like that."

WILLOW AND I RETURNED to our room, grabbing some food on the way for my rumbling stomach, and we spent all morning just... Talking.

I'd tried to just bury my feelings and move on from everything that had happened over the past few weeks.

Everything the Council did to me when they had me locked up, the way I felt when Maria had died, and my subsequent attempts to fix everything.

Or at least have it mean something.

And I'd tried to bury it all, just as I'd buried the years and years of failure and rejection that came before.

As if it couldn't touch me if I just refused to think about it.

In turn, Willow told me about growing up alone in her coven, taking refuge in her connection to her element, and daydreams of one day becoming a good enough Witch to show them all.

And as much as she swore she would never follow in her father's footsteps, she admitted that she always looked forward to his visits, saying that he saw her as the person she knew she was in a way that no one else did.

And that she never forgave him every time he left again.

She admitted how she'd finally found a home at Ember, just as I had, and how she'd hoped to finally prove herself here, where people didn't judge her.

And how the Amazons kicking her from their trials had brought that dream crashing to reality. And how her sorrow had swiftly turned to fury as she realised that it hadn't been because she wasn't good enough.

And that they were willing to kill me.

And then that fury had only been stoked by the Slayers' arrival, and then by the Council having her expelled.

Finally leading her to join her father.

And find the one place where she really was accepted and wanted.

As long as she was willing to kill for the mission.

I just curled up with her as she spilled all of her doubts that she had been too nervous to give voice to.

In case they stopped her from acting when she needed to.

We lost track of time, a knock at the door stirring us at late afternoon.

I headed to the door and opened it, seeing Freya beyond.

"Hey," she said. "I didn't mean to interrupt," I flushed as I remembered that I had changed into a pair of leggings and a loose fitting t-shirt, rather than real clothes, "but I just wanted to make sure that you were okay after yesterday. I'm guessing that you aren't up for training today-"

"No, I'm up for a bit," I said.

Willow was immediately beside me with a raised eyebrow.

"Just for an hour," I said. "Just to keep the routine somewhat consistent."

Freya smiled. "Okay, we can do a short training session and then maybe get some dinner. Damon's been craving sushi, if you want us to get some for you as well?"

"Yeah, that sounds good."

"Then meet Damon and I in the clearing when you're ready."

I nodded as Freya left.

"You sure you want to do this?" Willow asked.

I smiled. "Yeah. A little exercise won't kill me, and I should really apologise to Freya properly for yesterday. Also, now that she's said she's getting sushi, I really want some."

Willow smiled back. "Okay, then. We should probably get changed."

ONCE WILLOW AND I WERE in our armour, we headed out to the clearing.

We arrived to see Freya and Damon already there, waiting for us.

"Hey," I said as we approached. "Um, Freya? I just wanted to say... I'm sorry about yesterday. I got worked up, and I didn't mean to lash out, but I still did, and I'm sorry. I'll try to keep better control in the future."

The next thing I knew, Freya had her arms wrapped tight around me, holding me close.

"I don't need you to be better at pretending to be okay," she said before pulling away. "I need you to talk to me before you're not okay. When you hit me with your Energy yesterday, I felt everything you were trying to hide away." Her hand went to my shoulder. "I recognise those feelings, Amy, and they're not something you can just pretend out of existence."

"I know," I said. "I just... I wasn't sure what else to do. I didn't want everyone to think... To think that I couldn't do this."

"I know. And I know that you've probably spent too many years having to prove yourself. And not having anyone who understands. And I also know that it's not easy to let down your guard and open up. But trust me, it's worth it. And it might kill you if you don't. It nearly did me, and if Death hadn't sent me back... Well, let's just say that it's best to never get to that point."

I nodded, glad that Freya really did seem to understand.

And she wasn't freaking out like every time I'd tried to open up to my parents.

Nothing shut me down faster than the panic in my mum's gaze when I tried to admit how awful I felt.

And how quickly she went to blaming herself.

But Freya was just there.

Letting me know that she would listen if I needed.

"And Amy," Freya continued, "I know that I didn't hear this often enough when I was growing up, so, I love you. You're my little sister and you always will be, and that means that I'll always love you. That's not contingent on you being Angelborn or taking on the Council or anything else. Family isn't contingent on anything. It just is. And I'm always here for you. No matter what."

"Really? Even if this mess with the Council ends up with me labelled their number one enemy?"

"In that case, I will be doubly there for you. No matter what trouble you get into, Amy, you'll always have safe harbour in the Underworld. That I swear to you."

I nodded, not daring to do more as my throat tightened.

Freya smiled, apparently understanding as she turned to both me and Willow. "So, I've been thinking since yesterday, if the problem you girls have is that you don't have a bond, there are more temporary bonds you could use to help in combat. And given the nature of your powers, they might even allow you to share them, giving Willow the extra Energy reserves of an Angelborn and Amy the ability to control wind."

I raised an eyebrow. "Really?"

"Yes. You can only draw on powers that you have an affinity for – so Damon couldn't make the bond with me and draw on my elemental abilities – but I think your powers from Nature might be enough for you to be able to control wind if you're connected to Willow. I'm not certain that it will work, but it's worth a try."

"Definitely," I said, practically bouncing as I grabbed my wand.

Or, well, Maria's wand.

I guessed I was about to find out the hard way if it was as good at casting spells as my old one.

"So, how do we do it?"

"Hang on, I'll show you the spell."

Freya did, showing Willow and I how to draw runes on each other with our wands, the runes acting as conduits for our magic and allowing us to share it.

I went slowly and carefully, drawing the rune on Willow's bicep.

"Are you okay?" I asked.

"Yeah," she said with a smile. "Don't worry, it doesn't hurt."

I smiled in return, relieved that Maria's wand seemed to be working just as well as my old one had, allowing me to direct my magic into the rune with precision that such a delicate spell required.

Once I was done, I turned and allowed Willow to draw a similar rune on my arm.

As soon as she finished, I gasped at the rush of magic through me.

Connecting the two of us, binding us together.

It was temporary – I could remove the rune at any point and cut off the bond – but I could feel her just as clearly as I had been able to feel Natalie when she'd bitten me.

Willow smiled and I could feel it lighting me up inside. I couldn't help but smile in return.

Willow reached out for my hand, entwining my fingers in mine.

She bit her lip, and I was sure that she could feel the same thing I could.

I could feel Willow's hand in mine, but I could also feel my hand in hers through the bond, amplifying the sensation.

Creator, I wanted to kiss her and see exactly how much the bond would amplify.

Freya cleared her throat, drawing our attention back to her.

"As much as the bond can be used for other things, weren't we supposed to be focusing on combat training?"

I was sure I was bright red as I struggled to find my words through my embarrassment. "Right. Yes. Combat training."

Freya's smirk was a little too knowing as she turned to Damon. "How about we see what they can do now?"

Damon smiled, moving into position next to Freya as Willow and I both did the same opposite them.

Freya and Damon fought as competently as ever, but Willow and I didn't struggle as much as before against the strength of their bond.

No, I could sense exactly where Willow was at all times, I knew exactly when she needed me to strike or when she needed me to dodge.

And I could feel that she wasn't getting as exhausted as usual, able to pull on her magic more than she could before.

And when Freya caught me off-guard, I raised my hand and a blast of wind knocked her back several paces.

Freya grinned at that, shaking her head. "And I think with that display of elemental magic, it's time to call it a day."

I grinned back. "Why? Afraid we'll win this time?"

"No, I'm afraid that you might pass out. Willow's been drawing from your Energy reserves in this fight, remember? And that was your first time using elemental magic without a spell. You probably want to see how much it's exhausted you before you try to use it again."

I sighed, knowing that she was right but not wanting to admit it.

Not when I was finally winning...

"You did great," Freya assured me. "And once we're sure that you haven't drained yourself, we can pick this up again tomorrow." She then paused, her smile fading. "Or the day after, I suppose. I forgot, Esme's funeral is tomorrow."

I bit my lip at the thought. "Do you think there will be trouble?"

"When Sarah tries to expose the fact that Dana's lackeys are loyal to nothing but their own power? Yeah, 'trouble' is one word for it... Wear your armour and keep your weapons close. I doubt they'll just back down quietly."

I nodded, taking a deep breath to steel myself at the thought of tomorrow turning into a battle.

"Get some rest," Freya said. "I'll see you in the morning."

At that, she and Damon shifted away. Presumably back to their room.

I turned back to Willow, and she gestured to the path back.

I nodded, walking alongside her rather than shifting.

"So," Willow said, "are you sure you're ready for tomorrow?"

"I'm sure that I don't have a choice." I sighed. "But yeah, I'm ready. I'd rather face Dana's lackeys now than let the Council keep their grip on the Amazons even a moment longer. If the Amazons are the key to the loyalty of the Witches... Well, if we want to take the Council down for good, it would be best if they only had control of the Guides and Slayers."

Willow nodded. "I agree. Not to mention, that control won't mean much. I suspect that without the Witches, the Council will slowly crumble. We might not even have to fight them. They might destroy themselves."

"Do you really think that's likely?"

"Most of the time? No. But... Well, allow me one night of optimism before this all goes to shit in the morning."

I smiled. "Okay. I guess I can live with having an optimistic girlfriend for one night."

Willow shook her head, though she was smiling too. "I'm blaming this bond between us. It's not my optimism, it's yours."

I raised an eyebrow. "Have you met me? I'm not exactly a sunshine and rainbows kind of girl."

Willow then looped her elbow through mine, leaning close. "Okay, maybe 'your' optimism was the wrong way to phrase it. It's more... It's easier to be optimistic when you're with me. When I'm not alone."

"Yeah, I feel the same."

We kept close as we made our way back to our room.

As soon as I closed the door behind us, Willow turned to me, stepping close.

"So," she said with a smile, "want to see what this bond can do outside of combat?"

I smiled back before grabbing the front of her armour and dragging her close.

Our armour crashed together, Energy crackling as the bond told us that we both had the exact same intention.

We discarded our armour quickly, though I slowed as I was left in nothing but my underwear.

I'd seen Willow in her underwear, but we'd always been interrupted before I could get to that point.

I felt the urge to grab a t-shirt and cover myself up again, not sure that Willow would like what she saw, my hand going to scars over my shoulder.

Willow closed the space between us and kissed me softly. "You're perfect, Ni'tal."

I melted into her as she gently moved us over to the bed, laying me down beneath her.

Excitement and nerves crackled through me in equal measure and Willow paused her kisses, her hand going to my cheek.

"Are you okay? We can slow down if not."

"I'm fine," I assured her, my voice coming out breathless. "What about you? Are you okay?"

Willow smiled. "I'm more than okay right now."

At that, I kissed her again, my breath hitching in my throat as Willow's hands went to the back of my bra, fumbling for the clasp.

Irritation rose through me and I frowned.

Why was I irritated? It wasn't taking Willow that long to undo my bra, and I *definitely* wanted her to undo it.

Then I recognised the feeling for what it was.

Natalie.

The bond between us had been so quiet recently, I'd almost forgotten that it was there.

Which meant that I'd forgotten to try to shut it off before Willow and I had gotten carried away.

Guilt rose through me and Willow stopped her fumbling with a sigh.

"Natalie?" she asked.

I nodded, sheepishly. "She's annoyed that I didn't shut off the bond before..."

Willow just sighed again before lowering her head to my neck and kissing me gently.

I gasped, Natalie's annoyance unable to dampen my response to my mostly-naked girlfriend pressed against me.

"She's a grown Vampire," Willow said between kisses. "If she's annoyed by feeling your pleasure, she can shut it off herself."

I just nodded, my ability to think straight swiftly leaving.

"And you know what I think?" Willow continued. "I don't think she wants to shut it off. I don't think she's annoyed at feeling this. I think she's annoyed at herself for enjoying it."

I raised an eyebrow, my stomach twisting as I found myself unable to accept Willow's conjecture. "I don't know... Doesn't it make more sense that she's annoyed at the intrusion?"

Willow sighed, halting her kisses to face me properly. "Amelia... You're bonded to her, which means that you can feel what she feels. And you're also bonded to me, which means that I can feel what you feel. Which means that I can feel what Natalie feels. It's faint, but it's more than clear enough for me to see exactly why she's annoyed."

She then kissed me gently on the cheek. "And it's also clear why you can't see it. You're so convinced that she doesn't want you, and I have no idea why. She loves you, Ni'tal. It's obvious."

I shrugged, struggled to meet her gaze. "I guess I'm just so used to rejection, it's hard to see when it's not there."

"Well, if she wants to reject you – to cut off the bond – she can do so at any point. For now, let's just get back to where we were before."

Willow then returned her attention to finally removing my bra, and I lost all other thought to her kisses.

Every moment we were together, something in the back of my mind was waiting for Natalie to pull away.

To shut down the bond.

Only Willow was right, that moment never came.

In fact, I could almost feel her as if she was right there next to me, her hands on me as much as Willow's, her fangs gently trailing down my neck as the bond connected the three of us beyond what I had ever thought possible.

Eventually, when both of us were more than spent, I curled up against Willow, and in the moments before sleep claimed me, I expected Natalie to pull away.

To shut down the bond and pretend that none of this had ever happened.

And so I was thoroughly surprised when the response to that thought was a comfortable settling into the bond.

A letting go of the tension that had existed within it since Natalie had first bitten me, as she finally embraced the connection.

Chapter Six

I awoke with a smile the next morning, cuddling into my girlfriend, though my smile didn't last long.

No, not when I could also feel the familiar emptiness of Natalie having shut off the bond.

"Damn it," I groaned as I sat up.

Willow sighed as she too awoke and saw me.

"Natalie close the bond?"

I nodded. "Did we fuck up? I mean... Maybe I should have just closed the bond last night. Maybe I pushed her too hard, too fast..."

Willow sighed. "Again, she could have closed the bond at any moment. She chose not to. And it was pretty clear through the bond that she was happy with that decision last night."

"I know, but..."

"But she's as bad as you for letting her anxieties run away with her?" Willow snuggled up next to me. "Whatever am I going to do with the two of you?"

I raised an eyebrow. "You say that as if you don't mind that it's the two of us."

Willow just sighed again. "I knew that it would be the moment I saw that she had bitten you, Ni'tal. Either I let you go, or I accepted that you were now a package deal." She gave me a warm smile. "I think I made the right choice."

I snuggled further into her, hoping that she was right.

Though as much as I wanted to stay snuggled up with her for as long as possible, I knew that we were on a schedule this morning.

Presumably on the same page, Willow said, "Anyway, you'll see Natalie at the funeral, so... Well, that's probably not the best time to iron this out, but at least you'll be able to talk face-to-face instead of just sending your feelings to each other across the bond."

"Yeah," I said with a sigh as I got up. "I might not be able to talk with her *at* the funeral, but I'll probably be able to after. You know, assuming this doesn't all go to shit."

"I guess we'll just have to wait and see," Willow said, though her faded smile betrayed the fact that yesterday's optimism was nowhere to be seen.

We both knew we would be lucky if things didn't completely blow up in our faces today.

But there wasn't really much else we could except head out and face it.

"I'm gonna grab a shower and get dressed," I said, and Willow nodded before sliding out of bed and grabbing her own armour.

Yeah, this was going to be a long day...

ONCE WILLOW AND I WERE dressed in our armour, we made our way to the portal that Ms Griffin had set up to take us to Themiscyra.

We arrived to see that we weren't the only students preparing to go.

No, practically the whole school was there, all dressed in black combat robes or armour.

Willow nudged me and I turned to see that she was nodding over to where Lena, Charlotte and Natalie were standing.

We headed over to them, Lena spotting us first.

She immediately dashed over and hugged Willow tight.

"Damn it, Low, I haven't seen you in forever." She then pulled away with a glare. "Why haven't you come to say hi since you got here?"

"Oh... Um... I guess I've just been busy."

Lena folded her arms, clearly not buying it.

Willow sighed, looking away. "I just... I didn't feel like being told off for joining the *Fin'hathan*. I know that you've never exactly been a fan of theirs, and..."

Lena rolled her eyes. "And you thought I wouldn't want to be your friend any more. Look, Low, I don't think this is the best life choice you ever could have made – I kind of always figured you would join the Guardians with me when we left school – but I understand why you decided to take this path. And I'm not gonna stop being your friend over it."

Lena then turned to me. "And what's your excuse for the distance?"

I glanced to Natalie almost reflexively, and Natalie met my eyes just briefly before looking away, crossing one arm over her chest as she protectively held her other arm.

A cascade of conflicting emotions washed over me. Guilt came first, but it was twisted up around memories of last night. Positive memories of finally being able to let go, to not have to suppress her wants and desires out of a fear of biting anyone.

And then doubt. Doubt that the feeling was sustainable. That it wasn't just a one-time thing and that I wouldn't change my mind and decide that I only wanted Willow.

That doubt then led to frustration for letting her guard down, and then it looped back around to the guilt.

Guilt for having dared to get herself into that position in the first place, rather than shutting the bond down as soon as she'd realised exactly what Willow and I were doing last night.

I tried to reach out to her through the bond and reassure her. Yes, this situation was complicated and messy, but if I was going to leave her in the dust, I wouldn't have kept the bond open the night before.

This wasn't some game I was playing, and I wasn't going to lose interest and leave.

Before I could figure out if my effort to reach Natalie had worked, she closed the bond.

So, she had probably felt *something*, but if that something had gotten my point across was another question.

I was going to assume 'no'...

The crowd in front of us started moving before I could actually say anything, heading towards the portal.

Towards Themiscyra.

Lena didn't press me further as we moved along with the crowd, and I got the impression that it wasn't just because she was focusing on what lay ahead.

No, the sympathetic glances both her and Charlotte were giving me, Natalie and Willow said that my glance to Natalie had given them the answer they needed.

I hadn't been avoiding them, I'd been avoiding her.

And I was only doing that because Natalie had made it clear that that was what she wanted.

I suppressed a sigh as we finally reached the portal, refocusing on the task ahead.

I could talk to Natalie when we got back to the school that night, and we could finally sort everything out.

We passed through the portal and I felt the familiar sensation of a bubble popping over me.

We arrived in a corridor filled with portals, and more lines filing out, each being added to by several more portals, bringing in Witches from all over the world.

I frowned as I examined the crowds, though.

While they weren't small, I couldn't see anyone that looked over thirty.

We slowly moved out of the portal building, coming out to see that the surrounding buildings were decorated in black ribbons that seemed to be drawing in light, making the already dark winter morning bleaker.

But next to the ribbons were also candles, which were almost burning brighter for the presence of the ribbons.

The light in the dark. That seemed fitting. And the decorations were carefully placed, covering absolutely every building and surface possible, leaving the entire street dim and dark except for the bright specs of light from the candle flames, lighting the way to the funeral.

People had obviously set this up with care.

We headed through the streets, still following the crowds, and I saw several Witches off in side streets, not yet making their way to the funeral.

Probably Amazons who knew the island well enough to not feel the need to be early.

But the more I watched, the more I frowned.

The younger Witches were all in the same black armour or robes as me and my friends, but whenever I saw older Witches, I saw a lot of colour.

And a lot of casual clothes.

I supposed it made sense that not everyone would show up. Esme was a politician, and it wasn't as if I'd ever thought about my representatives in the Human world like this.

No, the younger Witches weren't just here for Esme the woman, but for the hope that she represented.

Another dash of colour caught my eye and I looked over to one of the side alleys to see two older Witches with almost identical blonde dye-jobs that were almost offensively bad given that they had access to magic.

But not nearly as offensive as the smirks they were failing to hide as they watched us make our way through the streets.

Their unrestrained glee at the thought that Esme was dead.

That all the young Amazons were grappling with the loss of the one person that had shown them that things didn't have to be like this.

They saw young women trying to desperately hang on to what remained of their hope with everything they had, and their reaction was to *smirk*.

Wind whipped around us, and Willow took my hand.

"Hey," she said gently. "Let's not cause a storm. Sarah has a plan, we just need to see it through."

I took a deep breath and nodded as I realised that the wind picking up had been me, channelling Willow's powers subconsciously.

Still, the deep breath didn't really help.

What could possibly help with witnessing that kind of cruelty?

I didn't have an answer, but given how often I'd been seeing it lately, it was probably an answer I needed, or the despair and rage that followed would swallow me whole.

Just like it had Maria before she'd found me.

My free hand went to my wand, for comfort more than anything – a reminder that I *could* do something if I wanted to, that I wasn't helpless, I was just choosing to trust Sarah – but after we saw a few more Witches talking, a spell from Maria's memory came to my mind.

One to help me listen in on the Witches in question.

I cast it silently, the spell a surprisingly taxing one for something I would have thought relatively simple.

I decided not to keep it going for more than a few minutes, but that was more than enough time.

"I just don't see why they've bothered with all of this fuss for Esme. She was barely in charge for five minutes before she got herself killed. Whereas Dana was in charge for years, and no one's even mentioning her death. She was the one who deserved all of this, not these smears that she was the one to kill Esme. If she stabbed her, it will have only been because Esme was ruining our people. Quite frankly, I'm glad that she's gone."

The wind whipped up around us once more, and the few loose strands of Willow's hair not braided up fluttered around her face as she sighed.

"Ignore them," she said, squeezing my hand.

"I know, but... How? How can they possibly think like that Willow? Their tone when they spoke of Esme..."

Willow leaned closer to me, the armour over our shoulders briefly knocking together. She sent reassurance back to me through the bond and I realised that she hadn't overheard the conversation.

Only I had.

Still, she said, "Let me guess, it was the same way people speak about Maria?"

I almost stopped dead in the street as I realised that Willow was right.

And that was in no small part responsible for my fury.

"I understand," Willow said. "This is why I took up my blade. I don't understand how people can be so callous and drive the rest of us off a cliff's edge with their hate-filled self-interest. They prefer Dana because they benefited from the status-quo and fuck all of us who were harmed by it. Esme never wanted to hurt them, just help us, and that was enough to justify her death. I couldn't just sit by and do nothing. But what I can do is wait for my moment, not start a tornado in the street."

I nodded, knowing that she was right, but also struggling to let go of the anger.

Waiting had never been my strong suit.

I focused ahead to see Lena looking back at us, apparently listening in.

She turned her attention to Willow. "You know, taking up your blade wasn't the only option. Lottie and I haven't just been sitting doing nothing, and neither have the young Amazons who supported Esme.

We're not ignoring any of this, we're just not letting our despair turn to violence."

"I wasn't the one who put the knife in Esme's back. The violence isn't just our doing, Lena. They just happen to have the sanction to do it. Which means that they'll keep doing it, and they will never be held accountable. You and Charlotte helped to get Esme rightfully elected, and they responded with a blade. It's time for something else."

I bit my lip. I didn't want Willow to be right.

The last thing I wanted was for Willow to be right.

But...

I just didn't know.

And given that Dana killed Esme – probably with the Council's sanction – did we have the time to wait and see?

Or would Sarah have the same target on her back the second she called the loyalty of the rest of the Amazons into question?

And did we let her die, or did we act first?

I honestly wasn't sure.

Thankfully, a large building loomed overhead before we could continue the conversation.

I was pretty sure that it was made of the same white stone as the rest of the buildings on the island, but it was covered in the same black ribbons and tiny candles that made it hard to tell, the entire building a glittering tower of lights that offered just the merest suggestion of columns between each floor of the circular building, going up for several floors.

There was a large entryway, allowing the crowd to pass through with little resistance.

We moved through into the entryway and there were more doors ahead, and stairs leading up on either side.

We were guided up the stairs to the first floor, but I got a good enough look through the entryway to see the room beyond and realise that we were in a repurposed colosseum, the stairs leading us up to more viewing areas, with a large platform in the centre.

Where a coffin lay.

I got a glimpse of Freya's onyx armour for just a moment before I lost sight of the door, standing in the front of the viewing area on the ground floor.

When we made our way up to the viewing area on the first floor, we managed to get seats in front and I immediately peered over the edge, looking for Freya's armour once more.

I found her, standing next to Damon, and two Mermaids I didn't recognise. One seemed even more inhuman than Lena, with no hair to cover her deep blue scales. Just a silver circlet encrusted with jewels.

The Mermaid next to her looked more like Lena – another hybrid I supposed – though she had a similar circlet over her deep blue hair. She wasn't standing like the others. No, instead, she was sitting in a wheelchair.

Charlotte cocked her head, her gaze on the same place as mine. "I didn't think the Atlantian royalty would show up."

Lena shrugged. "Lady Melody is half-Witch, so..."

"Still, it's just her and Queen Freya. You'd think the other factions would show some support."

"Like who? The Slayers and the Guides are under Council rule and the Council are the ones who did this. There aren't enough Elves or Dwarves on Earth to make a real community, and the Dragons don't leave their city for anything. That just leaves the Vampires and Werewolves, and they don't have any higher authority than the leaders of individual nests and packs, and individual pack and nest leaders would never presume to do something that might suggest the support of the whole. Like attending the funeral of a controversial political figure. That just leaves the Guardians, and all of their higher-ups are too close to Caroline and Persephone Raven to ever be able to be in the same building as Queen Freya."

I sighed at the realisation of just how alone we were in this fight.

Willow reached over and took my hand once more, reassurance seeping in through our bond.

And a reminder that just because some of our allies had to be silent didn't mean that they weren't there.

The *Fin'hathan* and the Guardians couldn't be here, but we knew that the *Fin'hathan* agreed with us, and it was more than likely that the Guardians did too.

We just couldn't ask them because of Freya.

Though, if we did have to choose, I would probably stick with my super powerful older sister.

I'm not sure I could bear to lose her again.

The noises around us seemed to settle, and I realised that everyone had taken their seats.

Sarah must have realised it as well, as she stepped up on to the platform and a hush fell over the crowd.

"Good morning everyone," Sarah said, a spell amplifying her voice so that the entire crowd could hear. "Thank you for coming. I know that Esme would have been heartened to see so many Witches coming together like this, though I wish it could have been under better circumstances.

"Those who know me will know that Esme was a close friend and mentor to me. I was so terrified when I arrived on Themiscyra, so scared that I wouldn't be accepted among so many elite Witches. I was a Healer and Esme was a Lorekeeper, but she soon took me under her wing and made sure that Themiscyra became a home to me, just as I know she did for many other young Witches over the centuries.

"The thing I will likely remember most, however, is how much Esme taught me about loyalty and what it truly means to help your people. I'd worked for the Council of Light in the past, thinking that I was helping my people. Thinking that antagonising the Demons was the only path forward. Esme helped me to see a different path. One that didn't seek conflict, and one that put the lives of other Witches above petty politics."

She reached for her wand and I tensed in my seat, my hands gripping the edge of the wooden bench.

This was it.

The point at which Sarah would ask everyone to say the oath.

And prove that most of those in leadership positions didn't actually care about what was best for the Amazons.

Just in protecting their own power and that of their friends.

But before Sarah could continue, the doors slammed open.

I stood up, drawing my own wand as I turned to the door.

Willow's hand went to mine, restraining me.

Presumably because she saw what I saw.

The Witch from the Council, followed by more Slayers than I had ever seen before.

And more than we could possibly fight.

Assuming they were here for a fight. The Slayers, thankfully, had their weapons still sheathed. Their presence alone was a threat, but I supposed they weren't looking for an immediate fight.

Which was why Willow was advising caution.

Right. Wait for your moment to strike and all that.

Only I could end up in a situation where having an assassin for a girlfriend got me into less trouble...

"Healer Sarah," the Witch from the Council said as she strode forward on to the platform, her voice amplified in the same way Sarah's had been, "I am here on behalf of the Council of Light to arrest you for conspiring to kill your fellow Witches."

Sarah just stared at her as Slayers marched up on to the stage. "I... What?!"

"You had the crystals around this island primed, ready to aid you in a loyalty spell. A spell that you had altered so that it would kill everyone who was revealed to not have been entirely loyal to Esme. Death to those who did not mindlessly fall in line with your cult leader."

"What are you talking about? I would never-"

"So you deny that you were going to use a loyalty spell just now? That you primed the crystals to make it more powerful?"

"Well, no, but I only-"

"There is no weaselling your way out of this one. The crystals were primed to kill."

Willow turned to me, muttering under her breath, "The Council will have altered the spell. I have no doubt that an inspection will show that they *were* primed to kill, and Sarah just admitted to priming them."

"But not for this. Surely a truth spell would-"

"Truth spells can be worked around. Especially by someone as mentally disciplined as Sarah. No, no one will investigate this further. The Council will say that they did enough, and pressing the matter will mean openly challenging them. No one with the power to actually hold them to account will do that."

"Are you sure?" I asked as Freya stalked up on to the stage, shrouded in flame.

At Sarah's other side, her husband did the same, drawing his sword in preparation to fight his fellow Slayers.

"**What do you think you're doing?**" Freya demanded. "**I was with Sarah when she primed the spell. There was no intent to kill.**"

"The spell was altered after the fact," the Council member said with an overly smug smile. "It seems your old friend used you as a witness, knowing that you would not be doubted. She tricked you as much as everyone here."

"**Yet all I have is your word against hers, and I trust hers over anyone else's.**"

"Freya," Sarah said, giving her friend a pleading look. "Don't. I'm not worth a war."

"You are to me."

Sarah gave her a small smile. "I know. I know, Freya. But I will not have that blood on my hands. Please. I'm innocent, we both know it. So, prove it for me."

Freya continued to glare at the Council member, but her flames died down.

Presumably because she knew that Sarah was right.

"All right," Freya said. "I swear, I will."

The Council member then turned to Freya shaking her head. "I'm afraid that we can't have you interfering with our investigations here on the island. Until we are done, you and all Demons are banished from Themiscyra."

"You can't-"

Freya disappeared in a flash of light, along with Damon and a small handful of Witches.

Natalie doubled over with a groan.

"Nat, what is it?" I asked as I dropped to her side, the bond reawakening between us and sending a cascade of pain through me.

"She banished Demons," Natalie managed to hiss through her teeth. "I don't think I have enough Demon blood to disappear, but..."

Charlotte brought out her wand. "It's your bond with Amelia. It's keeping you grounded. I can cast a spell to strengthen it, but if I don't..."

Natalie groaned once more. "If you don't, I'll have to leave. Just like Freya. But with her gone, we're the only ones left who can clear Sarah's name. Lady Melody is a hybrid married to one of the Mer King's youngest children, if she pulls Atlantis into this, it will mean her head, and the Amazons won't dare to defy the Council with their leadership in disarray. No, I have to stay. This is on us."

"Natalie, we can manage. If you don't want me to do this, don't feel pressured."

Natalie glanced at the four of us, and I knew exactly what she was thinking.

We were going to need every single person we could get for this.

She met my gaze and I felt the now-familiar cascade of conflicting emotions.

I bit my lip, knowing that I probably wasn't going to convince her just by telling her that I wanted her.

We didn't have the time for me to talk her down from her doubts.

"I think we both know that we're not going to be able to sever the bond," I settled for saying. "Not after last night. So I don't see how strengthening it can make things worse."

Lena frowned. "Wait, what happened last night?"

Charlotte sighed. "We don't have time for that right now." She turned to Natalie. "Are you okay with this?"

Natalie nodded. "Yes. Do it."

Charlotte nodded before placing her wand over Natalie's heart.

I assumed that she spoke the spell silently as her wand began to glow. Eventually, she pulled it from Natalie's chest, a thin rope of light still keeping it attached to her.

She moved the wand over to my chest, the rope of light leaving her wand to connect with me.

As soon as it did, Natalie's feelings washed over me with an intensity that I hadn't felt since she'd first bitten me.

But it wasn't the doubt or guilt that really hit me.

No, it was the loneliness and longing.

I wanted to grab her at that and hold her close and tell her that she never had to be alone again.

Neither of us did.

But Willow placed a hand on my shoulder, drawing me back to the present danger.

"If we're finished, we need to move. If the Council figures out that we're here, they'll banish us just as quickly as they banished Freya. Is everyone good to shift outside? To the café by the entrance?"

We all nodded, immediately shifting.

Once we were on the street outside, Charlotte indicated down the street. "Here. My place should be safe. I don't think the Council have ever actually seen me working with you, and I am still an Amazon. They won't let the Council just raid my home."

"Esme was an Amazon too," Willow said. "So was Sarah."

"No one was there to witness the injustice against Esme, and they set Sarah up pretty well. I doubt they've done that for me. And do you have a better idea?"

"No, I suppose not."

At that, we headed down the street to Charlotte's house, making sure to keep quiet and not draw attention to ourselves.

I wasn't sure whether or not to be thankful that the streets were still quiet. On the one hand, there were few people to see us, but if they did see us, we wouldn't just be another nameless face in a crowd.

"So, what are we actually going to do?" Lena asked as we walked. "I mean, we need proof that Sarah didn't mess things up, right? Well, won't we need to examine the crystals for that? Where even are they?"

Charlotte frowned. "I'm not actually sure. The Lorekeepers are in charge of them, but I haven't even written my first research proposal yet, so the Lorekeepers barely let me hang out in the more sensitive sections of the library. But... Maybe Katriona knows..."

"Katriona?"

"She's a Lorekeeper who worked with Sarah and Esme. We've talked a few times, and I think she could help us. She'd have access to the crystals, and she'll be able to help us actually examine them."

Willow frowned, tugging a loose strand of her deep red hair. "We probably need to get to her fast, then. If I were in the Council's shoes, I wouldn't let anyone who might be able to contradict my narrative just walk around freely."

Charlotte shook her head. "But that would mean every single Lorekeeper on the island. They wouldn't be able to keep that many people under their control."

"Maybe not, but I would rather not underestimate them. And even if they have to make a strategic decision, it will probably be to focus on the Lorekeepers who have been friendly with Esme and Sarah. Which would include your friend. Either way, we should get to her, and fast."

Charlotte nodded. "She doesn't live that far. Come on, it's this way."

She darted down a side street, and we followed close behind as the streets got narrower and more winding, the buildings getting taller.

Eventually, Charlotte stopped by a door, and knocked on it gently.

A rather disgruntled looking Witch pulled the door open with a glare. "What the hell do you want now-" She stopped, rubbing her left eye tiredly as she saw who was there. "Oh, Charlotte. What are you here for? You shouldn't be out right now. Come in."

She ushered us into the hallway, and I realised that there was nowhere to go but up the stairs to the upstairs flat.

The Witch led us up, Charlotte going just after her and the rest of us trailing behind.

"We were actually hoping to speak to Katriona. Is she home?"

The Witch turned to Charlotte with a frown. "You mean you don't know?"

"Know what?"

"You just missed her by about a minute. Slayers came by and demanded that she go with them. Apparently, Sarah was arrested at Esme's funeral?"

Charlotte nodded. "Yeah, she was. You didn't go?"

"No. Katriona's pregnancy has been giving her dizzy spells. They were really bad today, so I forced her to stay home. Fat lot of good that did when Slayers barged in here anyway. Apparently, they need to keep anyone associated with Sarah from interfering with their investigations, and that means all of the Lorekeepers. They might have taken Sarah's fellow Healers, too, but they're probably not as dangerous to the investigation as Lorekeepers."

Charlotte turned to Willow with a frown. "So much for not being able to capture and deal with all the Lorekeepers."

Willow turned to the Witch. "Do you have any idea of where they're being kept? If the Council rounded them up, it will be because they know the truth. If we manage to get them out, then we will be able to prove that the Council set Sarah up."

The Witch sighed, folding her arms. "I don't know, I'm not an Amazon, which is probably the only reason why they left me behind. I don't know enough about the island to tell you where they might be holding anyone."

Charlotte turned to Willow. "I might be able to see where they're being held. If the Council have captured this many people, all of their fates will be tied up in this. That's a hell of a lot of leads to follow."

Willow nodded with a sigh. "Okay. This is probably the best approach we have without any other allies on the island."

The Witch placed her hands on her hips. "I wouldn't say that you don't have any allies on the island, but none of us have the knowledge or skills to help you. The Council made sure that anyone both likely to help you and able to have been dealt with. We could maybe help you to overpower them, but... Well, I would rather you not get my wife in the middle of an all-out war in the streets."

Willow gave her a reassuring smile. "Don't worry, we want to do this with as few people hurt as possible. We're not going to rush into anything without being careful."

"Thank you. And if there is anything you think I can help with, just let me know. And I promise, I won't let anyone know that you're here. But you should get somewhere safe before anyone sees you. I doubt the Council will let you wander around the island if they realise that you're not at school."

We nodded before heading back out, all of us instinctively keeping close to the shadows as we made our way back to Charlotte's house.

Thankfully, no one seemed to see us, and as soon as Charlotte closed the door behind us, I drew my wand, Maria's memories supplying me with dozens of protective spells.

"Thank you," Charlotte said as soon as she realised what I was doing.

I just nodded, turning to her between spells to say, "It's no problem. You should get started on trying to figure out where the Lorekeepers are. Do you have any of the potions Freya gave you to help with your powers?"

Charlotte shook her head with a sigh. "No, I foolishly didn't think to bring them. I should have known that something was going to happen, and I might need to use my powers..."

Lena gave her a sympathetic look, allowing me to focus most of my energy back on casting the protective spells.

"We thought this would be an all-out fight if it was anything," Lena said, "and your powers weren't going to be helpful then. And last time you used them to look ahead for a mission, they... Well... Lottie, are you sure that you actually want to do this?"

Charlotte nodded. "I think the last time I tried to use my powers, I didn't have anything concrete to focus on. I had no idea what the mission ahead of us would look like, so trying to see it... Well, it's no wonder that my prophecies became vague and undefined. But I have a very singular question now, so it should come more than easily to me."

Lena sighed. "Okay, if you're sure."

I turned back to them with a frown, having finally finished all the protection spells I knew. "But that still doesn't solve the problem of you not having any of the potions that you used last time. Without them, how are you going to access your powers?"

Charlotte twisted her deep brown locks between her fingers. "Well, Freya did show me other exercises to help me focus. They will take longer than the potion did, but if I focus, they should still work. And maybe if I don't completely submerge myself in the powers, I won't lose focus as easily."

I nodded. "Okay. Is there anything you need the rest of us to do?"

"No. I just need some peace and quiet."

At that, she made her way over to the sofa in the corner of the room and sat down, closing her eyes and getting into a meditative position.

Lena made her way over, and in an impressive feat for Lena, she just sat silently beside her.

Natalie made her way out of the room and towards the kitchen.

I bit my lip, wondering if I should follow her. We really needed to talk, after all, and if this was going to take a while... Well, maybe this was the only opportunity we would get.

Before I could go, however, Lena was at my side and I suppressed a sigh.

Of course, she'd only managed to say quiet for a few moments.

"Hey," she said with a frown, her voice low so as not to disturb Charlotte across the room. "Look... I just wanted to make sure that we were all on the same page here."

I frowned. "The same page? About what?"

"About how this is going to get much, much worse before it gets better. And how I don't think we're going to get out of this unscathed. Look, even if we prove that Sarah's innocent, it will probably come at the price of openly defying the Council. We haven't clashed with them like that yet. Everything they've done... Well, they've justified it. And every time we've managed to stand up to them, it's been through finding loopholes in their own rules or it's been in private. If we openly fight against a Council member in front of all the Amazons... Well, even if we do it for a good reason, they're not likely to let us off lightly. Now, I don't care about that because I've always intended to join the Guardians. Plenty of their members are exiles or on the run from one faction or another. But Charlotte? She's always wanted to be a Coven Head. To prove that she can be. To pave the way for other Witches like her to follow in her footsteps. I don't..." She folded her arms and looked away. "I don't want to take that away from her."

"Lena... Have you asked Charlotte how she feels about this? What she's willing to risk? I mean, all of this mess is about who gets to be the leader of the Amazons. And Charlotte is the only one here who was actually an Amazon. The Council siding with Dana and allowing her to kill Esme affects her more than any of us. It's her rights they're trampling over by ignoring the democracy here."

Lena sighed. "The thing is... I know Charlotte too well. And I know that she will throw away what she actually wants in a moment if she thinks that it will help other people. I'm just not sure that she'll actually be able to live with that sacrifice a few decades down the line."

"That still sounds like a conversation you should have with her. But if she does decide not to fight with us, let her know that we won't hold it against her. Even this... Using her powers to find the Lorekeepers... That's more than we could have asked for, especially given how much she struggles with her powers."

Lena nodded. "Okay then. I'll talk to her as soon as she's done finding them." She sighed and then placed her hands on her hips. "Speaking of actually talking to people, what's going on with you, Natalie and Willow?"

I sighed, having no idea how to explain any of it. "It's... Complicated," I eventually settled for saying.

Lena raised an eyebrow, but before either of us could say anything else, Charlotte began to speak.

"Sword swinging, not the first life they've claimed and not the last, but the one that will extinguish any hope of change. If we try to free the Lorekeepers, Sarah dies. If we try to examine the crystals, Sarah dies. If we try to find other evidence of the Council's tampering, Sarah dies. If we try to lead our allies in a straight fight against them, Sarah dies. They intend to execute her, and they will not allow distraction from their goal."

I hurried over with a frown, realising that Charlotte's gaze was still unfocused.

She was still looking into the future.

"Charlotte, can we free Sarah from wherever the Council is holding her? If we free her, can we stay the execution? Can we buy ourselves enough time to clear her name before they execute her?"

Charlotte paused for a moment and I worried that she hadn't heard me or I'd broken her out of her trance.

But then she shook her head. "No. If we free Sarah, they will refocus on protecting their evidence." She flinched. "All six of us will perish by their blade."

My frown deepened and I bit my lip, knowing that we were probably running out of time before Charlotte woke up.

I looked around the room only to realise that Willow wasn't there. She would surely know the best way to handle this...

But I didn't have the time to find her.

So, what did I think she would do? Or what would Maria do? Or anyone who was more qualified for this than me...?

We couldn't choose between Sarah and the evidence... But what if we didn't have to?

"What if we split up?" I said. "I could go in to free Sarah while the rest of you try to find the evidence you need to clear her name. Would that work?"

Charlotte seemed to stay silent for an eternity and I worried my bottom lip until the coppery taste of blood filled my mouth.

"I think... I think..."

At that, Charlotte's gaze refocused.

"Fuck," she muttered before turning to me. "I'm sorry, Amelia. I saw enough to see that you and Willow managed to get Sarah free-"

"Willow?"

"Well, there was no way that she was going to let you do that part of the mission alone. I saw the two of you get Sarah free, and I saw the rest of us find the evidence we need. But I lost the connection before I could see anything further."

"Well, what else is there? I mean, if we manage to get Sarah free, and we manage to get the evidence, what else do we need?"

"Aside from getting away safely?"

I shrugged. "Look, if we can manage the rest, I'm going to assume that we will manage to get away."

Charlotte nodded, presumably following my logic.

"Do you know how much time we have?" I asked. "Before they execute Sarah, I mean."

"We have until noon tomorrow."

I frowned. "And that really wasn't enough time to get the evidence?"

Charlotte shook her head. "No, as soon as the Council realised what we were doing, instead of trying to stop us, they just went ahead with the execution. They have every important area lined with protection charms. Even with Maria's knowledge and Willow's training, we couldn't get past them without the Council realising what we're doing. But if we don't make our move, then they will wait until tomorrow. Until they can have the most witnesses for Sarah's execution."

"Which is why getting both Sarah and the evidence at the same time works. Okay, then that gives us tonight to prepare."

Charlotte nodded. "I'll make up some healing potions."

"Do you need a hand?"

"No, I can handle it. Not to mention, I think you have other things you need to deal with tonight."

I sighed, hating to admit that she was right. "Okay. If you need anything, let me know."

Charlotte nodded as I stood up before looking around. I had no idea where Willow had gone, but I probably did need to go over the plans for tomorrow with her. Though, I also needed to speak to Natalie, and I did know where she had gone...

I headed to the room next to the kitchen, with the door slightly ajar, assuming that Natalie had headed inside after she'd made something to eat.

But as I approached the open door, I realised that she was already talking to someone else.

I stopped outside the door as I recognised Willow's voice.

"-ever told you when I first realised I was in love with Amelia?"

I peered inside just enough to see Natalie raise an eyebrow. "I don't think we've ever spoken about your relationship at all."

Willow sighed. "Yeah, that makes sense. But maybe I should fix that." She leaned forward, her elbows on the dining room table as she got a far-off look in her eyes. "After the Amazons kicked me out of their trials, I had no idea where I was going or what I was doing any more. I knew that wanting to join them was an unlikely fantasy, but... It was all that I had. And then Amelia came along and she... She showed me a new way forward. As if it was effortless, she just forged her own path. *Our* path. A future worth fighting for."

Natalie looked down at her hands on the table for several moments before eventually muttering. "It was the same for me. I mean... I'd already *liked* her, but when we got to know each other, and I realised that maybe she understood... Maybe she understood how crap it all was and was also willing to fight for something better. It was a kind of hope I hadn't dared let myself have." Natalie then rolled her eyes. "And then all of the stuff with Maria... Creator, I never know if I need to let her go and conquer the world, or if I need to hold her close so that she doesn't get killed."

Willow smiled. "Yeah, I know what you mean."

I was about to storm in there and demand to know what they meant by that, when Willow sighed, turning to Natalie.

"You know, I always knew that Elves back in Skyreach weren't monogamous, but I didn't understand it until this whole mess. It's clear that we're both in love with Amelia, and she's in love with both of us. I don't think that needs to come with a sacrifice. I think we can make this work."

"I mean... I want to, Willow. More than anything. But are you sure? If it comes down to it, I know Amy will choose you over me. You were the one she *wanted* to bond with, I'm just the one who almost died and forced her into it. I don't want to let myself..." She trailed off, looking away.

"You don't want to let your guard down just to be hurt?"

Natalie nodded.

"I promise, I'm not about to change my mind on this, Natalie. Not least because I'm not actually sure that she would choose me. I only ever had a chance with her because you didn't risk starting a relationship. If you had, I don't doubt that she would have been patient with you until you both decided to bond."

Natalie gave a small smile. "It wasn't *her* patience that was the problem."

Willow smiled back. "Well, I guess it's not something you have to worry about now. Another reason to not be so sure that she would choose me. Though, as soon as we're done here, I absolutely intend to bond with her as well."

"Good. I hate the fact that things are uneven between us right now."

I finally decided to open the door and let them know that I was there.

"Hey," I said as I entered.

Willow's smile widened as she saw me. "Hey," she said in return while Natalie stayed silent, her cheeks turning pink. "Did Charlotte see anything?"

"Yeah. The bad news is that the Council intend to kill Sarah and will execute her the moment we try to clear her name. The good news is that Charlotte thinks that if you and I go to rescue Sarah at the same time as everyone else goes to get the evidence, we'll be able to keep Sarah safe and clear her name."

Natalie frowned. "Wait, just the two of you will be going to get Sarah? Surely, she'll be kept tightly locked up. And with Slayer guards."

I shrugged. "Charlotte thinks we can do it, and between Willow's awesome assassin skills and my Nature-sight and Angelborn abilities, I think we'll be fine."

Willow folded her arms. "Don't forget my ability to control air. Or your access to Maria's knowledge, which I'm assuming is good for breaking people out of prisons."

I grinned. "It is excellent for breaking people out of prisons."

Natalie's worried look refused to lift, however, and I felt more than clearly through our bond that she couldn't shake the thought that this wouldn't end well.

That she might lose me just as she'd finally reached the decision to let me in.

I tried not to smile at the realisation that she really did mean to stop pushing me away, instead focusing on the spell of Maria's that came to my mind. One that she had written when feeling the same way Natalie felt now, only about Helena.

"There's a spell that Maria used to use when she and Helena used a temporary bond similar to the one between me and Willow. It takes a few hours to prepare, but it should strengthen our Energy reserves by combining them further. I could set it up now, and then we could cast it between the three of us in the morning. It should give us an extra edge."

Willow smiled. "Sounds good," she said before turning to Natalie. "What about you? Are you in?"

"I... Yeah, I'm in."

⌘

I SPENT THE REST OF the day putting the spell together, thankful for Charlotte's well-stocked cupboards.

When I was done, Willow and I headed to one of Charlotte's spare rooms, deciding that an early night was probably best.

"So," Willow said as I closed the door behind us and started to remove my armour, "how long were you listening to me and Natalie before you came into the room?"

I raised an eyebrow. "You mean you don't know? I would have thought an assassin couldn't be sneaked up on like that."

Willow rolled her eyes. "What can I say, I was distracted."

"We're in enemy territory, babe. I don't think we have the luxury of getting distracted."

Willow raised an eyebrow. "*Babe?*"

"What? Am I not allowed to use a term of endearment for you?"

"Well, you are, but *babe?* It's not exactly *Ni'tal.*"

I sighed as I pulled on some pyjamas before flopping down onto the bed. "Is it really so different? I mean, *Ni'tal* could just be Elven for 'Babe' as far as I know."

A slight blush formed over Willow's cheeks as she looked away. "Ah... I guess I never gave you an accurate translation, did I?"

I shrugged. "You've always just said that it was a way of saying that you care about me."

"It is, but it's also a promise. Most Elven endearments are promises, actually."

"Oh? And what are you promising?"

Willow smiled softly as she looked me over and it was my turn to blush. "It depends on the Elf. Most are promising to protect and love and stand beside their beloved, no matter what. And then some also have specific promises as well, unique to their relationship."

I frowned slightly, butterflies appearing in my stomach as I took a moment to find the nerve to put voice to my thoughts. "Willow... Those sound like wedding vows."

Her blush deepened. "Well... They're not *not* that. But the 'Ni' prefix denotes that the promises haven't been formally made. It would be '*Yi'tal*' once they were."

I bit my lip, unable to resist the urge to tease her. "Well, I don't really have a term that works as proto-wedding vows readily available in English. Though, I guess if you truly intend to bond with me, like you told Natalie, I could always start calling you my bonded. Or would 'my wife' be better?"

I couldn't help but grin as Willow turned crimson at the term.

"I... Either," she eventually squeaked. "Either would be fine."

I just held out my hand, and she took it, allowing me to pull her down to sit on the bed next to me.

"So," she said, clearing her throat in an attempt to regain some composure, "you heard that much at least."

"I heard everything from you telling Natalie that you first realised that you were in love with me when you realised that I would fight for our future together. No matter what that ended up looking like."

Willow leaned forward at that, capturing my lips with hers as her hands went to my oversized t-shirt and gripped it tight.

I wondered if putting pyjamas on had been a pointless exercise.

"No one's ever been willing to fight with me before," Willow admitted as she pulled away. "I'd almost forgotten that I could."

"I felt the same."

Willow gently rested her forehead against mine. "I hope Natalie believed me when I told her that I want her to be a part of this. That she won't back away again."

"She won't," I said with a smile. "I can feel it through the bond. Can't you?"

"No." Willow sighed. "I think the bond is starting to wear down."

"All the more reason to make it permanent."

"I know. But... Let's just wait until after this battle, okay? Bonds can be overwhelming when first formed, remember?"

I sighed. "Yeah, okay, I remember. But the second we're done here..."

"Of course," Willow said before leaning in to kiss me once more, one hand threading through my hair as the other went to my waist, and she guided me to lie down beneath her.

Before we could do anything else, however, there was a knock at the door.

Willow groaned as she pulled away.

"It's Natalie," I mouthed as I felt her through the bond.

Willow perked up a little at that.

"Come in," she called, while not getting off me.

Natalie opened the door, only to turn a deep shade of crimson as she saw Willow sprawled over me. "Oh, um... I didn't mean to interrupt, I just..."

Willow finally sat up at that. "It's fine, Natalie. Come in. Did you need something?"

"I, um... I was just looking to talk, but... It can wait until after tomorrow."

"No!" I said before she could turn back to the door.

Natalie raised an eyebrow at the exuberance of my outburst.

Heat flooded to my cheeks. "I, um... I just mean..." I sighed. "You should stay. You should stay here with us tonight."

Natalie bit her lip, looking between me and Willow.

I moved back from her, realising what Natalie was thinking.

"We don't have to... I just meant that we should talk. Not anything else. Not if you don't want to. I just... As I said before, I don't think this bond between us is going to break. And I don't think either of us actually want it to. So... We should figure out what that means."

Willow nodded. "We should. And you need to drink from Amelia again, Natalie. You'll need your strength tomorrow, and if you enthral her properly, and not take as much as last time, it should be fine."

Natalie nodded, though it was a little hesitant.

I reached my hand out to her. "You don't have to if you don't want to. But I want you to."

At that, Natalie took a hesitant step forward.

"Okay," she said before taking my hand in hers, allowing me to gently lead her to join us.

Chapter Seven

I awoke with a smile the next morning, the bonds from both of my loves next to me resonating between us.

Though, my bond with Willow was noticeably weaker when compared to the one with Natalie.

That probably shouldn't have been a surprise, given that I only had a temporary bond with Willow, and my permanent bond with Natalie had been strengthened the night before, as the bittersweet ache on my neck reminded me.

Still, if we used the spell to strengthen the bonds, it should have a much greater effect on the bond with Willow – as that's the one that needed strengthening – and that should even it out.

I gently eased myself out of bed, not wanting to disturb either Natalie or Willow as I went.

Thankfully, they both stayed asleep as I made my way out of the room.

We had a nightmare of a day ahead of us, and they would probably need as much sleep as possible to face it.

I grabbed the pouch from my armour's belt before heading to the kitchen, careful with the door out of the bedroom as I went.

I briefly opened the door to the dining room on my way past, sensing that the spell we had set up there the night before was now fully charged, ready to strengthen our bonds.

I smiled before entering the kitchen and grabbing a glass of water before taking my medication from my pouch and taking one.

I'd been kidnapped, captured and stranded enough times to make sure that I always had some spares on me at this point.

As soon as I'd finished taking my tablet, a pair of cool arms wrapped around my waist.

"Good morning," Natalie said as I leaned back against her.

I smiled. "Good morning." The bond between us was crystal clear now that she'd bitten me again, and I couldn't help but raise my eyebrow and notice how close her lips were to my neck as I felt exactly what she was feeling. "How are you craving my blood again so quickly after last night?"

"In the same way you can crave dessert after a filling meal. But don't worry, I know that you need all of your blood for this mission today."

'Worry' was distinctly the last thing on my mind as the hairs on my neck stood on end in response to her breath tickling across them.

Natalie finally pulled away, and I turned to face her.

She gave me a sheepish shrug. "Sorry... We probably shouldn't do anything that might tempt me to bite you again."

"Can't keep yourself from snacking?"

"Well, I guess I'm going to have to learn restraint. There's always a period when a Vampire first starts drinking blood where they have to get used to it. It's not exactly difficult to restrain yourself from making poor choices when you don't have particularly strong emotional reactions. But that also means that I've never had to practice restraint."

"I don't think not practising restraint was ever the problem. I mean, you have always felt more than other Vampires. No, I think that you just used too much restraint over the years and trying to find a balance is the problem."

Natalie sighed. "You know, I think you're right... But we don't exactly have the time for me to learn right this second."

"I suppose not." I reached out to take her hand in mine. "But when we're done with this fight, I'll be right there with you while you figure it out."

Natalie smiled. "Thank you. And speaking of after this... What do you actually want to do once we're done with this fight? I mean, obviously we'll go back to school, but... Well, I could maybe do with a bit of a break."

"Yeah, I guess with everything with the Amazons, we never really got a half-term break, did we?"

Natalie shook her head.

"Well, I guess we're not really that far from Christmas now. I'm probably not going to go home for that, so..."

"I guess Willow won't be going home either?"

I shrugged. "That would be my assumption."

"Well, I suspect that my parents would be more than happy for the two of you to come back home with me. Especially now that we're bonded. Or if you wanted to, we could stay somewhere on our own..."

"Maybe we could spend most of the holiday on our own, just the three of us. We can see your parents for the important days. Assuming Vampires celebrate Christmas."

"Yeah, Witches tend to focus more on the winter solstice, but Vampires tend to just blend into Human culture wherever they are."

"Well then, I guess that's the plan."

Willow wandered into the kitchen at that point, running her fingers through her long hair to keep it from her face as she yawned. "What's the plan?"

I smiled as I turned her. "We're figuring out what to do for Christmas."

Willow raised an eyebrow. "You are?"

"Yeah. You know, once we're done with this fight... Well, we should probably spend some time together. Just the three of us."

At that point, my stomach twisted as I remembered the certainty Natalie and I had about going back to school.

Even if we dealt with the Council... Would Willow be able to come back with us? Ms Griffin probably wouldn't simply let the whole assassin thing slide.

And even if Willow could come back with us, would she want to?

I didn't bring any of this up and Willow just smiled. "Yeah, some time together sounds good."

I took a deep breath, figuring that the exact logistics of the situation could wait until we'd dealt with the Council here.

If we could just get the Amazons out from under their grip...

Willow must have sensed my feelings, even through our weakening bond, as she reached over and placed her hand on mine. "This is the hardest part of the fight, Amelia. If we can do this, if we weaken their grip on the Amazons and the Witches as a whole, the Council will fall from within."

I wished that I could be as certain of that as she was, but at this point it was just so difficult to imagine that it would be so simple...

And maybe it wouldn't be, but this was at least going to be the problem solved for now.

The end of this chapter.

I decided to refocus on the mission ahead. There was no point in speculating about what would happen after a victory when we hadn't even won anything yet.

"Come on," I said. "We should cast the spell to strengthen our bonds before Charlotte and Lena wake up. If we only have until noon... Well, we should act fast."

Both Willow and Natalie nodded, and I led them through to the dining room, the built-up magic of the spell causing a crackling sensation over my skin as we entered.

"So," Natalie said as she made her way over. "How exactly does this work?"

"You two need to be at two of the points here," I said, indicating three points in the circular design I had drawn on the floor the night before, after pushing the table and chairs off to the side of the room.

Natalie and Willow went to their positions as I grabbed the candles I had left there the night before, placing them in the appropriate places around the design.

I moved over to my own position and the magic of the room washed over me and caused every muscle in my body to tense, telling me that the magic that had been building was just waiting for my signal to release.

I focused on the candles as I silently cast the spell to light them.

Flames flickered to life in an instant and the magic that had been building all night suddenly rushed between the three of us, connecting us through our bonds and strengthening them.

I gasped as I felt both Natalie and Willow's magic coursing through me, struggling to see myself as a distinct entity, just like when Natalie had first bitten me.

It was a struggle that I swiftly gave up, finding comfort in the connection instead.

I had no idea how long the magic had coursed through us when the feeling finally faded, but my legs were aching from standing.

I looked between the other two and saw that their laboured breathing mirrored my own.

"Well," Willow said, obviously going for a casualness in her voice that she wasn't quite reaching, "that was... Something..."

Natalie smiled. "Yeah, definitely something..."

"How do you feel?" I asked the two of them. "I mean, I definitely feel stronger, but it's the two of you that have just been plugged into an Angelborn."

Willow smiled. "It's like when we first made that temporary bond. Only... Stronger."

Natalie nodded in agreement. "Yeah. Like it took the connection that formed when I first bit you and tripled it."

I smiled. "Yeah, you know, I think it's safe to say that it definitely worked."

I also can't help but note how right the sensation felt, the three of us connected like this.

Like we belonged together.

Like we always had.

Willow headed towards the door. "Come on," she said. "We should make sure that the others are up."

I followed her out of the room, and Natalie followed me.

We walked into the living room only to see both Lena and Charlotte already fully dressed in their combat robes.

"About time," Lena said. "You guys have been in there for, like, an hour."

I frowned. "An hour? Really?"

Lena nodded.

"Technically it was only about fifty minutes," Charlotte said. "But that was quite a long time. Did the spell work?"

"Yeah, it did. But I guess we should focus on what we do next before we lose any more of the day."

Charlotte twisted her long dark hair between her fingers. "I think I'm certain of where the Council are keeping the evidence of their tampering with the crystals. The spell used to do it required rare and expensive components. They can't risk destroying those components, so they're trying to clean away any evidence of the spell. But that's going to take another twenty-four hours, at least, so if we can get to the components before then..."

"You'll be able to prove that they were the ones that tampered with Sarah's spell," I finished for her.

Charlotte nodded.

"Okay, well, you, Lena and Natalie need to find those components. Willow and I will go and free Sarah to make sure that they don't jump straight to executing her once they realise what you're up to."

Lena frowned as she turned to me. "If you free Sarah before we clear her name... Lia, they keep looking for excuses to hurt you. If they can label you a criminal..."

"We're all taking risks right now."

"But the Council don't care about the rest of us as much as you. And the rest of us aren't the ones who are going to free Sarah. If we're caught trespassing, that will be nothing compared to actually freeing someone the Council intend to execute."

I shrugged as Willow stepped forward. "Well," she said, "the Amazons and Council already hate me, and probably already consider *Fin'hathan* to be criminals, so there's not much more getting caught will do to tarnish my reputation. And Amelia's got glamours, so she should be able to stay out of sight."

Lena folded her arms. "And if you can't?"

I shrugged again. "Then I guess it's up to you guys to prove that Sarah is innocent, and all I was doing was protecting her."

Lena sighed. "Yeah... It's that simple..."

Natalie turned to me and placed a hand on my shoulder. "Lena's right. The Council have it out for you, and if they see an excuse to hurt you, they'll take it. Be careful."

"I will," I said before leaning in to kiss her. Hoping that I conveyed just how much I cared about her.

Just how much I intended to make it back and see her again.

"Okay," I said as I pulled away. "We should head out before anyone realises we're here, or the Council change their plans."

Charlotte took a pair of glasses from the coffee table and passed them to me. "Here. The Council probably took Sarah's, and I don't think either of you know enough sign language to properly communicate."

"Thanks," I said, taking them from her. "Okay, I guess I'll see you all later."

WILLOW AND I PARTED ways with the others as we reached the colosseum where Esme's funeral had been held.

It seemed that the Council were keeping the Lorekeepers, and the evidence of their tampering with Sarah's spell, inside, as it was the largest building on the island.

The only place large enough to contain that many Witches.

Of course, it had never been intended to be a prison, and the Council were probably banking on the fact that the Lorekeepers wouldn't risk breaking out.

After all, they would have to believe that the Council was conducting an unfair investigation to want to do that. Even if they believed Sarah was innocent, they probably also believed that the Council's investigation would reveal that, and that they would then let her go.

Hell, they probably didn't even realise that the Council intended to execute Sarah when they found her guilty.

So, while the colosseum needed protection spells, it didn't need particularly strong ones.

Which meant that Charlotte, Lena, and Natalie should be able to slip past them with little problem.

Willow and I, however, had a much harder target.

After all, Sarah both knew she was innocent and knew that the Council weren't acting in good faith.

Which meant that she knew that they were likely going to hurt her, no matter what.

And that their investigation was a sham.

Which meant that she was much more likely to try to escape than the Lorekeepers.

And there was only one place on the island that could truly contain a powerful Witch.

Willow and I headed to the town square, in the centre of which was a large tower, the tallest structure on the island.

Maria's knowledge told me that that particular structure had existed since her time. The strongest prison that Witches had...

Of course, it barely ever saw any use. The Amazons were so committed to the myth that they were the best of the best of the Witches that they could never risk imprisoning an Amazon who did commit criminal acts.

The PR risk just wasn't worth it.

And since Amazons rarely ever let outsiders on to the island, it meant that the tower barely ever saw use.

Sarah had probably been the first prisoner it had seen in decades.

I turned to Willow as we settled into a side street opposite the tower. "So, how are we going to get into a prison that is protected by some of the strongest spells known to Witches?"

Willow shrugged. "Well, I do have a few methods for sneaking into heavily guarded places, but I thought breaking into prisons was Maria's speciality."

"Technically, breaking out of prisons was her speciality, but I take your point." I frowned as I thought through Maria's knowledge, searching for anything that might help.

"I can temporarily pull the protection spell away from a small section of the building, allowing us to slip through without raising the alarms."

"How draining is it?"

I sighed. "I've done it once before... But it almost killed me."

Willow frowned. "I don't like the idea of you draining yourself so quickly."

"If we don't even get into the building, it won't matter how much I've drained myself. And this was way back when I first learned about my magic, before I even knew who Maria was. It's how I got Helena's grimoire. Since then... Well, I've bonded with Natalie, got a temporary bond with you, Maria gave the portion of her magic as well as her knowledge, and Nature awakened the part of my magic that was tied to her, so I doubt it will drain me that badly this time."

Willow sighed. "I suppose, even without all that, you would still be better practised with magic. But that doesn't mean that this isn't going to be draining, and if we need to get past any more spells to get inside..."

"Well, are any of your *Fin'hathan* tricks less risky?"

Willow frowned for a moment before reluctantly shaking her head. "I guess not. Everything else has a much higher chance of us getting caught."

"And if we get caught before we even get to Sarah, this is all over."

"Okay, I guess you're right. If we sneak around the side door, are you ready?"

I nodded. "Can you keep a glamour over us until we get through?"

"Yes, but I also need to maintain it once we get inside. There are probably guards."

I frowned. "According to Maria's memories, the protection spells on the tower are so strong that they never saw the need for guards."

Willow raised an eyebrow. "I take it this is one of the prisons that she broke out of in her time?"

I shrugged. "She was in here a couple of times, actually. But they were both when she was dating Helena, and I don't think it was necessarily a break out as much as the Amazons just didn't do anything to stop them, given that they didn't want to get into a war with the Demons."

"Does that mean that they had her under looser protections?"

"No, I don't think so. They just didn't try to stop her when she escaped."

"But if Maria broke out a few times, surely they then strengthened their defences?"

"They did, but I also have Maria's knowledge about those adjustments. And adjustments that they made between then and when Maria came back. This is one of the few prisons that she actually had a bit of trouble getting out of. She was quite diligent about mapping out her potential escape after that."

Willow nodded, seemingly happy with that.

Happy enough to go ahead, given that we didn't really have a choice.

Even if we weren't happy with this information, we still had to press forward. We couldn't risk the Council keeping Sarah any longer.

Willow cast a glamour over us, and while it wasn't as strong as any of mine, it was more than strong enough to keep people from seeing us if they weren't specifically looking for intruders.

We darted across the courtyard, taking advantage of the winter sun barely making its morning appearance, and the long shadows it cast.

Once we reached the side-door, I felt the familiar static of protection spells before us, and I pulled out my wand, steeling myself for what came next.

And doing everything I could not to think about the pain and exhaustion of getting Helena's grimoire.

I cast the spell silently, reaching out with my wand to take hold of the edges of the protection spell around the door, gently pulling without tearing it completely away and alerting the Council to our presence.

The spell pulled back with more force than I had been anticipating, and I had been anticipating quite a bit.

Mr Stiles was a powerful Demon, after all, and he had been protecting a book that none of the Demons wanted anyone near.

I'd figured that the protections on the tower would probably be stronger, but I wasn't prepared for the force with which they tried to snap back into place, resisting me at every turn.

I clenched my teeth, a thin sheen of sweat forming over my brow as I worked, slowly dragging the protection spell away from our entry point, my knuckles white around my wand.

"Amelia..."

I shook my head, hoping that Willow got the message not to distract me.

I almost had it.

"Now," I hissed as soon as I had a big enough gap.

Willow nodded and opened the door just enough to slip through.

I followed as fast as I could, trying to outrun the spell which snapped back into place as soon as I moved.

There was no way I could get through the door and keep the protection spell in place at the same time.

I gasped for air as soon as I was through, knowing that I had to sense if we'd managed to get through without disturbing the protection spell.

If not, there was a chance that the Council knew we were there.

That I had messed up.

But even with the urgency of my task, I couldn't force my body to do anything except gulp down more air, nausea and dizziness blocking out any other sensation.

"Okay," Willow said, her words the first thing to break through the haze of exhaustion crashing over me, "it looks like we managed to get through without disturbing the protection spells."

I nodded as Willow's hand went to my shoulder and I took some steadying comfort in her touch.

"Are you okay?" she asked. "I mean, I know you're not just through the bond. But..."

"I'll be okay to continue on," I managed. "Really, Willow. I'll be fine. I just need to catch my breath."

Willow nodded as more of my awareness came to me.

I was bent over, my hands resting on my knees, but I pushed myself up to a standing position, forcing myself to take slow, deep breaths.

Eventually, I had my breathing back under control and I looked around the room.

Thankfully, there weren't any guards.

If there had been, I wasn't quite sure that I would have been able to stay silent when I'd barrelled into the room.

Or even not managed to crash into them, as I realised that I'd stumbled a good halfway into the room after going through the door, which Willow had now shut behind me.

Thankfully, the room was empty except for a spiralling stone staircase, making its way up to the top of the tower.

"I guess we make our way up," I said.

Willow peered up the stairs before turning back to me, her form becoming more and more distinct as I got used to seeing through her glamour. "Can you use your Nature-sight to see if there's anyone upstairs?"

I nodded before doing as she asked. The tower was almost blinding with the protection magic woven into it, but I could still make out one distinct form.

Sarah.

I really hoped that the faintness of the light she was giving off was just because it was next to the blinding light of the tower.

I turned back to Willow. "There's just one person, and I'm pretty sure it's Sarah."

Willow nodded before heading upstairs first. I followed behind, glancing back every once in a while to make sure that we weren't being followed.

The stairs seemed to go on forever and soon my breathlessness wasn't just from getting past the protection spell. In all honesty, I would have suggested shifting the rest of the way if it wasn't for the fact shifting when you weren't entirely sure of your destination was dangerous, and Maria's memories told me that there would probably be defences in the tower against shifting.

Finally, we made our way to the top, and saw that there were six cells, though only one was occupied.

Willow dropped our glamour as we approached Sarah's cell.

I shuddered as I saw Sarah sitting in the corner of the cell, pale and covered in a fine sheen of sweat.

"Sarah," I said as soon as I saw her. "What happened?"

Sarah pushed herself to her feet, leaning heavily against the wall as she turned to us. "Amelia? Willow? What are you doing here?"

"The Council is setting you up, and they are determined to make sure that you don't make it out of here alive. We can't let that happen, so Charlotte, Lena and Natalie are going to find the evidence that we need to clear your name, and Willow and I are going to get you out of here."

Sarah frowned at my lips and I cringed, before passing her the glasses Charlotte had given me.

She took them weakly and put them on.

"Sorry," I said. "I forgot."

"Well, at least you brought them. I caught something about Charlotte and Lena... I think."

"The Council is setting you up so that they can kill you. We're getting you out of here while the others find the evidence to clear your name."

"If you're getting the evidence to clear my name, why do you need to get me out of here?"

"Because once the Council realises what we're doing, they're going to execute you. They'll give up on any pretence of a fair trial and just get it done. Charlotte looked into the future and she saw it. We need to get you out of here. Now."

Sarah sighed, and I could see that she was reluctant.

Probably because if the Council's plans weren't as dire as we were saying, her escaping would only cause more trouble.

But I couldn't quite pull my focus away from just how haggard she looked. "Sarah... What have they been doing to you?"

Sarah chewed her lip slightly before responding. "Magical beings with enough mental fortitude can fool truth spells. The Council wanted to make sure that their investigation was thorough, so they decided to wear down any resistance I might have, so that I won't be able to fool them. Not that they needed the truth about my spell, given that they set me up. I think they meant to get information from me about Esme's other supporters, not to mention Chris, Freya, and the Guardians. For someone who used to work for the Council, I'm certainly friends with a lot of their enemies."

I shuddered once more as I realised what she meant. That they had been torturing her. "I'm sorry."

Sarah shook her head. "It's all right, Amelia. I've been through worse."

"We need to get you out of here," I said as I made my way to the cell's lock. Thankfully, after all the protection spells from the outside the building, this one was a fairly simple locking mechanism that Maria had known how to get past.

I unlocked the door and Sarah stepped out, only to stumble as I realised just how shaky her footing was.

Just how shaky she was in general now that she couldn't lean against the walls of her cell.

Willow and I both rushed over to her, helping her stay on her feet.

"Come on," I said softly. "Let's get out of here."

But as we reached the top of the stairs, I saw a barrier of Energy sizzling across it.

Willow groaned. "It must have activated when you opened Sarah's cell. Another safeguard to make sure that she didn't escape."

"Okay, I think I should be able to break it. I just need to...."

I reached down to the barrier, my wand outstretched, but as soon as I got close, it reached out with swift tendrils of magic and grasped onto three of us, holding us in place.

"Well, well, well," came a familiar voice, "what do we have here?"

I fought against the tendrils just enough to crane my neck and see the Witch from the Council approaching us from the other end of the room.

Where she must have shifted in.

She sighed as she looked over the three of us, placing her hands on her hips. "Well, that's disappointing. I had hoped that Sarah's rescuers would be Queen Freya or that husband of hers. Or maybe even both."

Sarah glared at her. "Creator... This was just a trap. You were trying to lure in either Freya or Chris so that you could eliminate one or both of your two most powerful opponents."

The Witch shrugged. "*Three* of my most powerful opponents. Don't discount how problematic you've been to the Council's plans, as we know that Esme likely wouldn't have taken power without you and you have a real chance of being named her successor. Or, at least, you *had* a real chance of it." She sighed. "Between your influence here, Queen Freya leading the Demons, and your husband vying for the leadership of the Slayers now that Michael is out of the picture, the three of you had a real chance of creating an alliance that could have ended the Council. But not any more."

She turned to me, looking me over for a moment before sighing. "Well, Queen Freya might not have come for her best friend, but she might still come for her sister."

I just stared at her. How did she know Freya was my sister? Nobody knew that...

My shock must have been evident on my face, as the Witch smirked. "Really, Amelia, did you think you are the only one with the help of a Seer? She couldn't tell me exactly who would come for Sarah, but she knew that it would be someone of value. Either Freya, Chris, or Maria's protégé, who is apparently Queen Freya's adopted sister. Her little rescue of you after Maria's execution suddenly makes a lot more sense." She shrugged. "Regardless, I knew that whoever would come for Sarah, it would be someone of value. So now, I suppose we go back to waiting."

A chill went down my spine as I realised that the second Freya knew that Council had me in their grasp again, she would come for me. There was even a chance that she was already coming for Sarah, the Council's banishing spell the only thing keeping her from the island.

And if they meant to lure her back here, the banishing spell was probably one Freya could get through with enough time, a trick to rile her up, not something to truly keep her away.

And she'd had nearly a day.

As powerful as Freya was, the island wasn't her turf, and the Council were expecting her.

As soon as she showed up to rescue us, the Council would kill her. Just like they did Maria.

And just like then, I would be used as bait.

It would be my fault.

Dark Energy crackled over my skin as I did everything I could not imagine the Council running a sword through Freya, just like they had Maria.

And just like then, I would be bound and helpless to stop them.

My Energy flared further as I focused on the tendrils keeping me bound.

I couldn't let them hold me here. I couldn't let them use me like this.

I couldn't let this happen again.

I poured all of my Energy into the spell keeping me trapped, giving it everything I had.

I had to get free.

I was so focused on breaking the spell to see the Witch's knife until it was too late.

I doubled over in pain as the blade slipped through the plates of my armour and pierced my abdomen.

"Now, now. We can't have that. Stay still and stop fighting. I don't want to have to kill you before your sister can get here."

That solidified my resolve, and I poured every ounce of pain tearing through me into my magic, tearing at the spell that bound me, Willow, and Sarah.

Enough sense managed to seep through the pain for me to realise that I should focus my efforts on Willow.

As injured and exhausted as we both were, Sarah and I would likely only collapse once we were free.

But Willow still had a chance.

The spell eventually began to snap away from around Willow, every ounce of my pain only weakening it more.

"Dammit," the Witch growled before grabbing her wand and aiming it at me.

I focused everything I had on breaking Willow free before she could cast a spell, and a moment later I fell through the ground, the Witch's spell releasing me into the air, before I landed, several feet later, on a wooden floor with a thud.

Wait? Wooden floor? The tower had been made of stone...

I coughed, trying to force myself up into a seated position, though the stab wound in my side quickly told me that was a bad idea.

"Amelia? What are you doing here...? Creator, is that a stab wound?"

I frowned as I recognised the voice and a pair of hands went to my abdomen, slowing the bleeding.

"Somebody get a healing potion. And a teacher."

"No!"

Wind raced through the room and I finally recognised that I was in the dining hall of Ember Academy as the sudden gust slammed the doors shut.

The girl holding my wound closed, Claire, frowned at me. "What do you mean 'no'? Healing potions will help, but you really need to see someone. And where have you been? No one has seen you, Charlotte, Lena and Natalie since Esme's funeral."

"We never came back. The Council don't intend to play fair. They're going to execute Sarah, no matter what. We stayed on the island to get her out of there, and clear her name, but... It was a trap. The Council have Sarah because they want to lure in either her husband or Queen Freya. If you tell them I'm here and I'm injured... They'll walk right into the trap."

I had no idea how much sense I made, the words slurring through my pain, but no one seemed to be trying to open the doors as someone passed me a mug full of healing potion.

I pushed myself to sit up and downed it in one go, the wound finally closing as I felt a little less like death.

I pushed myself to my feet, grabbing a piece of chalk from my belt and immediately staring to draw a portal back to the island.

"Wait, what are you doing? You can't possibly intend to go back there. Look, the healing potion stopped you from bleeding out, but you can barely stand."

I shook my head. "I have to get back there. I managed to break Willow free from the spell that we were under, but... She's fighting a member of the Council on her own. I can't leave her there."

Claire nodded. "Okay. I'll go with you."

I frowned at her. "You don't have to do that."

"I don't have to, but if the Council intend to kill Sarah the same way they killed Maria, and intended to kill you... Not to mention Willow and Charlotte and Lena and Natalie... Well, you must think pretty poorly of me if you think I'll leave my friends to face that alone.

And that's before we even get to the fact that you won't even be able to get back to Themiscyra without help. It's highly protected, and any portal you try to make to get back will need to be strong enough to break through those defences. Even as strong as you are, I don't think you can break through on your own."

I frowned. Maria's knowledge told me that she was right, but I didn't want to drag anyone else into this.

"All right," I eventually said. "I guess you're right."

She turned to the rest of the dining hall. "Who else is coming with us to free Sarah from the Council and clear her name?"

To my surprise, pretty much everyone in the room – which meant a couple of hundred Witches – either stepped forward or raised their hand.

Claire turned to me with a smirk. "Then I guess you'd better draw quite a big portal. Here, let me help."

I nodded, passing her a spare bit of chalk as I refilled my cup with another healing potion. I could use all the help I could get...

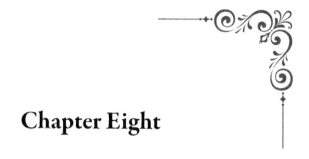

Chapter Eight

Ten minutes and a few more healing and restorative potions later, we had finished the portal, and I no longer felt like death.

No one had disturbed the doors, and I took that as a sign that no one intended to get any of the teachers, who had thankfully steered clear of the dining hall during breakfast, but a few of the girls had shifted back to their rooms to change into combat robes if they had them. Or to gather a few more friends that they thought might want to come along.

I turned to Claire. "We need to go soon. I don't want to leave Willow alone a moment more than necessary. Or risk any of the teachers figuring out what's going on here."

Claire nodded before turning to everyone in the room. "Okay everyone, let's light up the portal and go."

I took a vial of Faerie dust from my belt and opened it as all the girls in the room pointed their wands at the portal.

The wands began to light up one by one, and I watched carefully, waiting for the exact moment that everyone connected their magic to the portal.

We had to make sure it had enough charge to get us through the island's defences, but if we charged it too much, we risked overloading it and destroying the portal entirely.

I poured the dust onto the portal as soon as I was sure we were ready and held my breath, hoping that we had done this right.

After a moment, the portal lit up, rapidly expanding to fill the space.

"Okay," I said, turning to the girls next to me. "We need to be quick. I have no idea how long this is going to hold."

Everyone nodded and I jumped into the portal, confident that they were behind me.

We arrived just outside the colosseum, and several Slayers who were stationed outside immediately sent bolts of electricity cascading towards us.

Claire and I ducked for cover and I turned to her as several other girls retaliated against the Slayers. "Charlotte, Lena, and Natalie are inside the colosseum, trying to find the evidence of the Council's tampering. The Witch on the Council said that she had a Seer helping her and that's how she managed to figure out that Willow and I would go to free Sarah. If she knew that..."

Claire nodded. "She might also know that the others are trying to get the evidence."

I nodded. "You have to find them and make sure that they succeed. Free the Lorekeepers if you can, if you tell them the truth they will probably help." I then shrugged. "At the very least, they will properly fight to keep you and the other students safe."

"Okay. Where are you going?"

"To make sure that Willow and Sarah are okay."

"On your own?"

"I don't think I can get anyone else past the protective wards and into the tower."

Claire nodded. "Okay. I'll see you when this is all over."

"Yeah, see you then."

At that, I rushed back towards the tower, glamouring myself, so I wouldn't be seen by the Slayers, though they were now more than distracted by the gaggle of schoolgirls who were more than happily knocking them onto their arses.

I sprinted to the tower, nearly crashing into the side door as I went, only remembering that crashing into the protection spells would probably alert the Council to my presence at the last moment to stop myself.

If I tried to destroy the spells by brute force, or just ignore them and barrel inside, the Witch from the Council would know that I was back.

And that might give her the upper hand.

I focused on the door again, but it was difficult to keep my mind on-task. I still hadn't managed to fully recover from the magic I'd used earlier, and the familiar exhaustion of overusing my powers was starting to settle into my bones. Using such a powerful spell again was the last thing I wanted to do, but I had to, so I clenched my teeth and held my wand tight as I once again pulled away the protective spells surrounding the tower.

I had no idea how I actually managed it, but I stumbled back into the tower as my vision faded in and out.

I clenched my hands into fists and leaned forward, resting them and my weight on my knees, willing myself not to faint.

I had to get to Willow. I had to help her.

I caught my breath before forcing myself up the stairs once more, taking a moment to down some of the restorative potion that I'd attached to my belt in the dining hall.

I needed to be in a fit enough state to help Willow.

There was no point in going to help her only to be a burden.

I arrived at the top of the tower to see Sarah kneeling by the stairs, her wand out as she occasionally threw out a spell, though it was clear that it was draining what little strength she had left.

I followed the path of her magic to see two figures, moving faster than my eye could track before I fuelled my magic into my senses.

Willow and the Witch from the Council.

The Witch was keeping her distance, trying to hit Willow with spells.

Spells that were hurting her, if the blood dripping from her armour was any indication.

I cringed as the Witch spoke once more, throwing out another spell that Willow managed to dodge, but I recognised the spell through Maria's memories.

She was trying to bleed Willow out, using spells that encouraged blood to flow more freely from her wounds. Wounds that I suspected her other spells were causing. Spells that likely pulled no punches.

The Witch started to slow, however, and I realised the spells Sarah was throwing out were meant to keep her sluggish and keep her from completely overwhelming Willow. But with how little Energy Sarah had left...

I focused on Sarah, passing her a healing potion and a restorative potion.

"Amy?" she hissed under her breath. "You're back? How? Is Freya-"

I shook my head. "No, I made sure she doesn't know. I don't think any of us want a war here."

Sarah nodded. "Thank you," she said as she downed the potions and I refocused on Willow and her fight.

She and the Witch were moving so fast an attack seemed risky, so I focused on Maria's knowledge, hoping that she'd had at least one healing spell up her sleeve.

I didn't have any plants or anything to draw from for elemental healing.

My memories immediately went back to the times Maria had healed me. Healing had never been her strong point, but given how strong Maria's strong points were, that wasn't nothing.

I felt bad for my doubts as I remembered that she'd spent years leading her coven.

Looking out for them and healing their wounds as much as they'd healed hers.

Even Maria hadn't truly been alone her entire life.

Of course, healing spells required Light Energy, which I had never been good at drawing from.

But as soon as my breath got shorter with panic, reassurance washed over me.

Natalie.

She could feel my panic through the bond.

My worry that I couldn't help Willow.

You've got this. I'm here.

Light Energy rippled over my skin in a way that only Dark had before.

Ready for me to fuel into any spell.

Including a healing spell.

I reached out with my magic, focusing my Light Energy on Willow.

She glanced at me as soon as my magic hit her, and her whole face lit up as she smiled.

She didn't give the Witch she was fighting enough time to figure out what had happened, however, as she pushed forward, our bond telling me exactly what she intended to do.

And exactly what she needed me to do.

I got behind the Witch, keeping out of her sight.

Willow was relying on Maria's memories, hoping that it gave me a spell to trap an opponent.

And she was right.

I started weaving one such spell as quickly as I could, but I feared that I wouldn't be quick enough. These kinds of spells required time and patience...

Something we didn't have a lot of right now.

Still, every time the Witch threatened to turn my way, or turn in the direction I needed to go to set up the next rune, Willow diverted her attention, keeping her occupied as I slowly made my way around the edges of the tower walls, drawing rune after rune.

I finally began to draw the last one, and as I did so, the Witch turned her gaze from Willow for the first time, presumably realising that she was being led around in circles.

And she turned her gaze on me.

"*You!*" She drew her wand out at me, and I braced myself for whatever spell she had in store.

A single syllable left her mouth, however, before she was cut off by a cry of pain to her throat as she stumbled forward.

A knife in her back.

I refocused my attention on the rune, despite my worry for Willow as the Witch turned on her once more, focusing everything I had on drawing that last rune before the Witch realised exactly what we intended.

I held my breath as I finished the design and poured my magic into it, waiting to see if the gamble had paid off.

Magic crackled between the runes before reaching out and trapping the Witch, leaving her barely able to move.

I sighed a breath of relief, collapsing forward onto my knees as Willow approached the Witch with her dagger drawn.

"I'm going to make sure that you never hurt anyone ever again," Willow growled, but before she could get close, the Witch flicked her wand and the ground shook beneath us as my ears rang with the sound of a thousand blasts through stone.

Sarah pushed herself to her feet, making her way to the one window at the top of the tower, staring in disbelief.

She turned back to the Witch. "You set off explosions all around the island... You must have used the crystals. You must have set them up when you were setting me up. But why? There are innocent Witches on this island, the chances of none of them being hurt..."

The Witch smirked. "I didn't do anything. Maria's little protégé did. At least, that's all anyone else will believe."

The tower shook once more, and Sarah turned to me. "If she's setting you up, the explosions will be concentrated here. She intends to take all of us with her."

I didn't hesitate, knowing through the bond that Willow was following me as I grabbed Sarah, pouring all of my energy into shifting us out of there, despite the tower's defences.

The world fell out beneath me in a dizzying spiral, and it seemed to take forever to reform into anything familiar.

Maybe we hadn't gotten out of the tower fast enough. Maybe it had collapsed beneath us, and we were hurtling towards the ground.

Or maybe we had shifted out, but without a firm destination in mind, we had ended up trapped in an endless void of nothingness, falling for eternity.

The hard stone ground knocked the wind from me as we fell onto it, but I collapsed onto it with relief, choosing to ignore the blood seeping through my scrapes.

We'd hit solid ground. We were safe.

"What the hell has she done?"

I finally looked up from the stone cobbles beneath me at the sound of Sarah's voice, looking up to see that the stone buildings that had surrounded the tower were now crumbled to dust.

My stomach twisted as I hoped with everything I had that no one had been in there.

I gave the area a quick look over with Nature's sight and saw nothing, which was either good, or very, very bad...

Before I could think of anything to say, there was another blast behind me, and the next thing I knew, Willow was grabbing both me and Sarah, dragging us across the courtyard.

"Move!"

I obeyed as best I could, my feet stumbling behind me as Willow pushed me forward and I just leaned into it.

We made it to what was left of a side alley before we were knocked forward by another blast.

I coughed as dust filled my lungs, every bare scrap of skin on my front scrapped bloody by my landing, and my elbow throbbing in a way that I was sure was more than just bruised from my landing.

I forced myself to my feet, knowing that breathing in this much dust couldn't have been good for me.

I grabbed Sarah as I went, Willow's grip going to my shoulder to help me as we moved out of the dust just as the clouds settled.

I ran my hand on my uninjured arm through my hair, brushing away the dust as I turned to the site of the blast.

The tower was now a pile of stone.

I looked over it with Nature's sight, seeking any sign of the Witch.

But there was nothing.

Just like the rest of the rubble surrounding us.

"Shit," Willow muttered, staring at the wreckage. "Amelia... Sense the magical signature of the blast. What does that feel like?"

I frowned, doing as she asked.

My frown deepened as I realised what she meant. "It feels like *me*. Like my magical signature. How?"

"I'm not sure, but I'd put money on it having something to do with what the Council did to you when they had you trapped. Maybe they tapped your Energy to charge source stones."

My stomach turned to ice. "They kept exhausting me... If they took that Energy..."

"And then amplified it with the crystals, yeah, it's no wonder everything collapsed."

I turned to her. "Willow, if the remnant of the blast feels like my magic..."

"She wasn't just trying to take us with her. She was trying to frame you."

Sarah shook her head. "No. I won't let her. I was there, I saw what happened."

"Except you're a criminal at the minute as well."

"Just until your friends clear my name. Which means that we should probably go find them."

I nodded, suppressing a groan as every one of my muscles ached at the thought of moving.

But I knew that we had to press on.

"We should find the others," I said. "The faster we can find them, the faster we can clear Sarah's name. And if the Council used the crystals to frame me as well, they might have done it the same way they framed Sarah. We might be able to clear my name, too."

Willow nodded before heading towards the colosseum, me and Sarah following her.

We only made it to the end of the street before several Amazons in full leather armour shifted around us, their wands drawn.

"Stop right there," the one in front of Willow said, and we did as she asked, stopping dead, as the end of her wand glowed slightly. "What the hell is going on here?"

She immediately looked us over, her eyes narrowing as she saw Sarah.

And then her gaze went past us to the rubble behind.

She turned back to us, pointing her wand directly at my chest. "*You.* You destroyed the town square."

"I didn't do anything!"

She didn't listen, a rope of light shooting out from her wand to wrap around me, holding me in place.

Pain shot through my elbow as the rope held the injured joint at an awkward angle.

Willow drew her dagger at the pain as it cascaded through our bond, her blade at the Witch's throat before anyone else could realise what she was doing.

"Let her go," Willow growled. "Now."

The Witch glared at her, and I tried to push against the spell keeping me trapped as I realised that this would only escalate.

"Stop!" Sarah said, limping forward, towards the Witch. "Eve, please, this is a misunderstanding. Amelia and Willow are friends with a Seer who realised that the Council never intended to give me a fair trial. They came to free me, but it was a trap. Councillor Evans was there waiting for them, and when it became clear that she wasn't going to win the fight, she was the one to blow up the square. Not Amelia."

Eve frowned, looking between Sarah and the ruins behind us several times. "Sarah, with all due respect, the wreckage reeks of this girl's signature."

"Just as the Council claims that I cast a spell to murder half of the Amazons. You don't truly believe that, do you?"

"Well, no."

"But someone set me up, using the crystals. Why is it so unlikely that they would do the same to Amelia?"

Eve chewed the inside of her cheek before sighing. "It's not, but just because I think you're innocent doesn't mean that you are, and even taking you at your word... This doesn't look good." She then turned to me and scrutinised me for a moment before lowering her wand, the spell dissolving and letting me free. "But you don't look like you're in any fit state to cause real harm."

She then turned her gaze to Willow, glancing down at the blade still at her throat. "Are we good?"

"For now," Willow said before finally putting away her blade. "Is there any chance you'll let me cast a healing spell on Amelia? She's in a lot of pain."

"No. The fact that she's barely standing is the only reason why I'm comfortable with her walking around at all right now."

Eve turned to Sarah before Willow could argue. "We need to know if the Council really were setting you up or not."

"I believe Amelia's other friends were looking into that."

I nodded. "They went to the colosseum where the Council are holding the Lorekeepers. It's also where they were keeping the components they used to alter Sarah's spell."

"Then I guess that's where we're heading."

The Amazons kept a tight circle around the three of us as we moved, making sure that we didn't have the chance to escape if we tried.

Not that I thought that would be a good idea. My elbow was now refusing to move, leaving me holding my arm across my chest, unable to straighten it.

Willow turned to me as she tucked a loose strand of dark red hair behind a pointed ear, worry seeping through our bond.

Worry for me.

"I'm fine," I told her beneath my breath. "Really. It barely hurts."

"I can feel everything you feel, Amelia. I know that's not true."

I gave her the best shrug I could manage with only the use of one arm. "Okay, so maybe it hurts a bit. But it's far from the worst thing I've ever dealt with."

Willow shook her head. "That somehow doesn't make me feel better about the situation."

I suppressed a sigh, knowing that her worry was warranted but also wishing that she would just play along with my attempts to joke about the situation.

It was about the only thing keeping me going, keeping my focus from the fact that the very skilled warriors surrounding us were pretty sure that I had not only killed a member of the Council, but levelled a huge part of their city.

Eventually, we made it to the colosseum, seeing a group of fellow students from Ember Academy casting spells similar to the one Eve had just used to tie me up.

Willow turned to me with a raised eyebrow and I gave a half shrug once more, though this one was a little more stilted, my arm losing more and more movement with each passing moment.

"I might have brought some help with me when I came back," I said, under my breath once more.

For the first time in what felt like forever, Willow managed a small smile.

"Amelia!" Claire came running over to us. "You managed to get Sarah out of there. And it looks like you have friends." She turned to the Amazons surrounding us. "Are you here to help out? I think we've got it mostly under control here now."

Eve took a moment to respond, just staring at the girl in front of her as she searched for an appropriate answer. "We... We're just here to make sure everything gets sorted out."

"Oh, well, I think Charlotte, Lena and Natalie are with some of the Lorekeepers, examining the components the Council used to frame Sarah. I can take you to them if you want."

Eve nodded. "Thank you."

Claire smiled. "No problem. Just follow me."

We followed as Claire took us through into the colosseum, seeing both Lorekeepers and Ember Academy students helping heal each other's wounds throughout the space, the healthiest of them keeping eyes on the captured Slayers.

Rather than taking us through to either the stage or the stands that we'd been in the day before, Claire took us through to a back room, where our friends were waiting for us.

"Amy!" Natalie said with a grin as we approached, relief washing over me through our bond as I realised that she had been able to feel my pain as we'd been approaching, worry eating away at her as she'd been trying to just focus on the fact that I was alive.

She stepped forward, though stopped as her gaze fell on the Amazons surrounding us, her eyes narrowing as she looked them over. "What's going on here?"

Eve placed her hands on her hips. "We're just here to find out exactly what's going on."

Natalie's scrutinising gaze didn't let up as she answered. "Well, Charlotte and Katriona are looking over the components now."

"Katriona," Sarah said, perking up.

Natalie nodded over to the far side of the room, and we followed her gaze to see Charlotte looking over several pieces of what looked like bone, along with an older Witch in Lorekeeper robes.

Eve approached, clearing her throat, and that seemed to be enough to alert the two women to the presence of the Amazons in the room.

The older Lorekeeper, who I presumed was Katriona, turned to Sarah with a smile. "Ah, Sarah. I didn't think they would get you out so fast, but I'm glad that they did. I can't imagine being locked up was pleasant."

Eve raised an eyebrow. "Get her out?"

"Yes. Because she's innocent, obviously. Charlotte and I just finished examining the components a few moments ago, and we sent a couple of the Lorekeepers to the tower to get Sarah free." She then looked over the Amazons escorting us. "Though as I said, I hadn't anticipated them getting to you so quickly. Or getting the help of anyone who wasn't on guard duty..."

"No, we weren't on guard duty. I was simply nearby when the entirety of the town square blew up. I was searching for survivors when we came across Sarah and these two girls. Apparently, the destruction happened while getting Sarah free."

Katriona's face fell. "Ah, I see. Well, as I said, it's probably a good thing they did free her, given that she wasn't in the wrong here. It does seem as if the Council altered Sarah's spell using these components. Sarah never meant to do anything except show who was truly loyal to the Amazons, and who among those we had chosen to lead us were more focused on personal gain. Actually killing anyone who was highlighted for hypocrisy was something added later. As I said, it seems the Council set her up with the intention of keeping her out of power."

"Did you find any other form of tampering with the crystals? They were used in the destruction of the town square, and they reeked of Amelia's magic. Everyone here is claiming that the Council faked Amelia's signature to set her up."

Katriona frowned. "No, I'm afraid we haven't found anything of the sort." She turned to me and Sarah. "Do you have any idea how that might have happened? How exactly do you think they framed you?"

I hugged my injured arm tight to my chest. Or, at least, as much as I could without hurting myself. "They held me captive for a while, saying that they were examining my magic, but whatever they did exhausted me thoroughly, several times. They might have been charging source stones from my magic."

Katriona gave me an apologetic look. "I'm sorry, Amelia. If they used source stones to power the spell through the crystals, there's no way to trace it. Even if we found the source stones in the rubble, I doubt they would hold any of your signature any more. Though, I suppose if we did find some..."

Eve shook her head. "That won't be enough evidence, and you know it. Not with how many Amazons were still in those buildings."

The room spun as my stomach fell out from beneath me.

I really had hoped that those buildings had been empty.

But if they hadn't...

There hadn't been anyone left to sense within them after the blast.

The Council hadn't just framed me for property destruction, they'd framed me for mass murder.

Eve turned to me. "Amelia, if we don't have enough evidence to prove that you're innocent of this... Look, it seems that the Council weren't above framing Sarah, so I can't definitively say that they didn't frame you too. But people will be out for blood after this. The best I can do is give you time to get away from here before I tell anyone."

Sarah stepped forward, glaring at Eve. "No, I won't allow this. Amelia didn't do anything wrong, and I was there to witness it."

Eve shook her head. "And for anything else, I think that would be enough, Sarah. But it truly may not be here."

Katriona turned to Sarah as she stepped forward. "Eve's right, Sarah. I understand you want to defend an innocent girl, I truly do, but I think you should also consider the fate of the Amazons as a whole."

"The fate of the Amazons as a whole? What do you mean?"

"I mean that you truly do have a chance to be named as Esme's successor. It was a long-shot before, given your youth, but now that the Council have stooped to trying to frame you, I don't think that anyone who supported Dana, and by extension them, will have much support going forward. At least for a short time. I think you might have the slight edge here. But if you defend Amelia..."

I swallowed, willing back tears as I realised what they were saying. "If she defends me, she'll probably lose enough support to lose her edge over other opponents. And the Amazons will go right back to being under the rule of someone who is loyal to the Council."

Sarah turned to me, her gaze filled with determination. "Amelia, me winning the leadership won't mean anything if I didn't stand up for every Witch, including you. You're innocent, I can't just stand by and let them blame you for this."

"You have to," I said, my resolve hardening with every word. "You have to, I won't let you do otherwise. Won't let Esme's legacy die here. Not over me."

I couldn't help but look over to my friends at that. I was deeply aware of everything Esme had meant to them. Of everything the hope that she had brought meant to them. Lena, Natalie, and Willow had all been excluded from the Amazons for not being Witch enough. And

Charlotte was setting her entire life up around proving that she was as good as any of them, regardless of what they thought of Litcorde.

Esme's leadership had meant a future where they didn't have to fight to be respected by their fellow Witches. By the Amazons.

Esme's leadership had been based around fighting for a future where they didn't have to fight for their place among the Amazons. Where they were accepted for who they were, with no caveats. And as the Amazons set the example for all the Witches across the world, it would have really changed things.

Now there was a chance for Sarah to continue that, how could I possibly ask them to give that up for the sake of Sarah defending me?

How could I ask every Witch like them to give it up?

Every Witch like me.

If I didn't do this, if some Witch loyal to the Council took over, I would still be screwed.

Never able to fully trust the Amazons or any coven once I graduated from Ember Academy...

Well, if I was going to be an outcast either way, what did having people think me a criminal really change?

I turned back to Sarah, and she simply nodded, understanding in her gaze.

She knew just as much as I did how much my friends needed this.

Sarah then turned to Eve. "Well, regardless of what's going on with Amelia, if we have established that I'm innocent, and also part of the interim leadership until we figure out who should truly succeed Esme, then I think that it's important that we establish now that the girls who helped us here are welcome among us. After all, if they helped to both prove my innocence when the Council of Light – one of the most powerful magical organisations in existence – would attempt to set me up, and they also managed to subdue an army of Slayers, I think they've proven themselves worthy of the Amazons."

It took a moment for me to realise what she was saying.

That Lena and Natalie, despite Dana's trials deeming them unworthy, would now get to be Amazons.

They would have a home here, just like Charlotte.

There probably wasn't a better way for Sarah to establish exactly what kind of leader she intended to be going forward.

It took a moment for Eve to process her words, probably not expecting that out of the previous conversation.

Eventually, she nodded. "I suppose you're right. We will need to convene the leadership to make it official, but I don't think anyone will object."

I felt Natalie's shock through the bond as she tried to process what had just happened.

Lena managed to process much faster, however, stepping forward. "What about Willow? I mean, she helped get Sarah free from the Council, didn't she? She's included in this too, right?"

I wasn't sure that Eve had even known Willow's name before that point, but Lena pointing to her made it more than obvious who she was referring to.

Eve turned to Willow, and her gaze simply rested on the dagger at her side.

"She did, indeed, help to get Sarah free. But that freedom came at a cost, and we can't know what role she played in all of this. I doubt she will be blamed for the blast in the same way Amelia will be..."

Willow placed her hands on her hips. "It's okay, you can say it. The Amazons will never accept an assassin within their ranks."

Lena frowned, but Willow cut her off before she could protest. "Lena, it's fine, really. I would never leave Amelia, anyway."

At that, Eve turned to me. "Speaking of, there is only so long I can go without telling everyone what happened. And only so long before others stumble across the ruins of the town square. Especially if Katriona sent Lorekeepers there to find Sarah. I think you had better go."

I nodded, and Sarah turned to me. "Amelia... Do you have somewhere you can go? Aside from Ember Academy, I mean. If the school wants to remain on good terms with the Amazons..."

My stomach churned as I realised what she was going to say. And that she was right. As much as the school had become a home to me, I couldn't go back there.

They couldn't be seen to be harbouring a fugitive.

No one could. Not my auntie, not the school, not Freya...

"It's okay," I managed. "I have somewhere where I can lie low for a while."

I had no idea how long 'a while' would actually be, and I refused to think on it.

That was a problem for later...

I took Willow's hand before shifting us out of the colosseum, into the nearest patch of nature.

The edge of a forest at the end of the city.

Eve was right, we had to go.

"Amelia, wait!"

I turned, stunned to see that Natalie had followed us.

She approached with a frown. "You're not really going through with this, are you? I mean, how can you be sure that they will find you guilty? You didn't do it..."

I shook my head. "People will be looking for someone to blame, Nat, and they will have two options. Blame the dead Councilwoman that most of them still probably revere, or blame the living girl who was the protégé of Maria Brown. Without Sarah to defend me as an eyewitness, all I have to speak in my defence against the abundance of magical evidence against me is..."

I stopped, not wanting to say something so harsh, but Willow took a slow, deep breath before finishing for me.

"All she has to speak for her is me. The *Fin'hathan*. And no one will take my word seriously."

I cringed, wishing that her words weren't true.

I must have broadcast that thought through our bond as Willow sent back a wave of reassurance.

She'd known that this was the price of her taking up the blade her father had given her.

But that didn't make it right.

Still, I refocused on Natalie, knowing that she wasn't quite ready to give up. "Nat, even if Sarah did speak up for me, I'm not sure that it's a fight that could be won. And as Katriona said, it would likely do more to erode Sarah's legitimacy than actually defend me.

"I know what I'm doing here, Nat. Really. I can't let Sarah throw everything away just to try defending me."

"Then I'll defend you! Amy, you can't-"

I cut her off before she could continue, making sure to stress through our bond how much I met my next words. "You can't throw away your future, either. I won't let you."

"Even if I don't defend you, I'm not staying here. I'm coming with you."

"No, Natalie, you can't. You need to stay here. The Amazons need you and the others. They need you just as much as they need Sarah."

Natalie shook her head. "They can make do without me."

"Maybe they can. But... Natalie, you should stay. Willow and I... We will never be accepted here. No matter what. You still have a chance."

"A chance that doesn't mean anything without you."

"I'm not saying to let me go forever. I'm just saying... I can't ask you to become a fugitive with me. And right now, the task that's ahead of the Amazons won't be easy. Sarah is going to need help to set them on the right path, and I don't trust anyone to do that more than you."

Her eyes shone with tears. "Nothing I say is going to change your mind, is it?"

I shook my head. "Not a single word."

She bit her lip. "Do you really have somewhere safe to go? Somewhere they won't find you?"

"I do. Maria left me quite the hiding place. Not to mention, I've got a friend who owes me, and a promise to keep."

Natalie nodded, though it was clear that she was looking for an excuse – any excuse – to make me stay.

But we both knew that there wasn't any.

"Make sure that the Amazons stay on the right path," I said. "And when they no longer need you, come and find me. I'll be waiting."

"I'll be there as soon as I can. I swear."

At that, I stepped forward, closing the space between us and kissing her one last time.

The bond between us echoed with the unwillingness of either of us to go.

And the bittersweet knowledge that we had to.

"I swear, I'll do everything I can to make my way to you again as soon as possible," Natalie said as she finally pulled away.

"I'll hold you to that."

Natalie smiled slightly as I stepped away, retaking Willow's hand in mine as we stepped through the treeline, and into Nature's clearing.

Away from Natalie.

Willow placed a hand on my shoulder. "You okay?"

"I will be," I said. "For now, let's just get home. I need to take something for this." I nodded to my arm.

She hesitated, and I knew that she wanted to press me, to make sure that I was okay with leaving Natalie behind.

The truth was, I wasn't, and I think we both knew that.

So, she didn't press, she just nodded as I led her back out of the clearing and towards Maria's tower.

We made our way up the tower silently, and I found an old healing potion on the shelf, downing it in one.

As my elbow slowly repaired itself, Willow turned to me. "So, what did you mean when you told Natalie that someone owed you a favour? And that you had a promise to keep?"

I shrugged. "Well, I did make sure that Councilwoman White's daughter didn't lose her child. I figure she probably owes me now, which might give us an in with the Guardians. Out of any faction, they're probably the only ones who will ever speak to us now."

"Probably. But even they probably won't be so keen to talk to you in the immediate days after the Amazons accuse you of destroying the centre of their city."

"I know. Which is why we should probably focus on the promise I made. I told Maria that I would help to free her coven, and I intend to keep that promise. So, are you with me?"

Willow smiled. "Always. Though, if that was something even Maria struggled with, it will likely be quite the undertaking."

I nodded. "And by the time we're done, it will probably have been long enough that the Guardians will be willing to talk with us. Maureen might have mentioned that they had some plans that they may need an Angelborn's help with. So, if this all sounds good to you..."

"It does. Though, there is one thing I want to do first."

She stepped closer to me, taking my hands in hers.

I raised an eyebrow. "Oh? And what's that?"

"To finally bond with you. What do you say?"

I simply closed the space between us, allowing my magic to flow through the temporary bond between us as it became permanent.

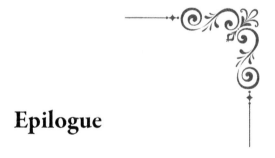

Epilogue

Jessica ran her hand through her long, mousy hair as she went through her nightly ritual of organising her notebook.

Of sifting through every piece of information she had collected on her niece's whereabouts.

It had always been enough over the years to know that Amy was safe. That she was alive and healthy, and attracting trouble all over the place.

But anything more than that?

She was always gone too fast for Jess to track her. She was practically a ghost.

And if Jess was being honest with herself, things were probably better that way. If she couldn't track Amy, it meant no one else could, either.

But still, she wished that she had more.

She was pulled from her thoughts by her bedroom door opening, and Gail stepping through with a yawn.

"Ready for bed?" the other woman asked as she placed a gentle hand on Jess' shoulder.

Jess sighed. "Yeah," she said, finally turning from her notebook to face her wife. "How is the new school year shaping up?"

Gail groaned.

"That bad, huh?"

"Not awful, just... Get ready for some real handfuls in class next year. Including the Raven twins."

Jess smiled. "I think I can handle two Litcorde Demons. I'm just glad that we're finally expanding beyond Witches. It will be nice for the students to see what the rest of the magical world is like."

Gail returned her smile, warmth radiating from her gaze. "I agree. At this rate, I was worried that we would still be struggling to expand the school by the time our children attended."

Jess raised an eyebrow. "*Our* children? When did we decide on that?"

Gail sighed, not returning Jess' joking tone as she pulled her hair from the bun on her head. "Are you truly still worried about what Nightingale will think? Jess, it's normal for Witches to have several rounds of children. And Nightingale is old enough to be starting a family of her own soon. I don't think she'll really think she's being replaced."

Jess sighed as she stood up and made her way over to her wife, taking her hands in hers. "I know, but... Just let me handle this, okay? Her being an adult doesn't necessarily mean that she won't worry that a new child is replacing her. Not to mention, as Witches, we've still got decades left to have children. There's no rush."

"No, I suppose not. But still... I think we both know that nothing in life is certain, and I don't want to bank on time we might not have."

Jess simply sighed once more, having to agree with that sentiment. "I'll talk to her next time I see her," she eventually said.

Gail smiled. "Sorry, I didn't mean to get all doom and gloom. And actually, I had some good news to tell you."

"Good news?"

"I heard a rumour today that the Guardians finally managed it. They finally cast a spell across their home city so that Humans leaving will lose any memory of magic. They made the whole city a safe space to tell Humans the truth about magic."

Jess took several moments to process what Gail was saying.

If that was true, it was huge.

And something that would require the power of an Angel.

Or something close to it.

"Did Freya cast the spell?"

"No, it doesn't look like it. No one knows who it was."

Jess couldn't help but smile. She knew exactly who it had been.

She let out a sigh of relief. It had almost been too long since Amy had appeared from the woodwork.

But no, she was out there, and she was fine.

And that would be enough for Jess to sleep that night.

Want to read more? You can download a free short story following the end of this book at: lcmawson.com/EAEpilogueShort

Dear Reader,

A nd that's the end of the series!
　　　Wow, that's really weird to say... I don't think I'd really realised that this was my last time really with this manuscript before sending it out until I actually typed the words.

But yeah, I guess this is the end of Amy's story. At least, it is for now. Like all Snowverse characters, she'll be around for other stories.

And if you want more time with other characters from Ember Academy, I'm currently working on a new series that's also going to be set at the school, though several years later.

As of writing this, I'm only part-way through writing Book One and just have a teaser up on my website, but I'm hoping that by the time most of you read this – so, you know, people reading on Amazon, not my Patreon supporters, who will get it in a couple of hours from writing – the pre-order for Book One will be up for you to check out, and maybe even the free prequel novella will be available.

You can check it out at: lcmawson.com/ember-academy-for-magical-beings

Special Thanks

I just wanted to give a shout out to my Patreon supporters as well as everyone who has left reviews of my books!

My Patreon supporters are a massive help to me being able to do this as my job (or, well, one of them... Cue a joke about being a millennial in this economy while I cry over my two degrees...) and reviews are a massive help to me being able to do this emotionally.

Seriously, they make my day and everyone who has left one deserves cookies!

Want to Keep in Touch?

If you want to connect with me and other fans of the series between books, I have a weekly newsletter where we discuss things like the best fantasy soundtracks to work to and which vampire lore is the best, and there's also a closed Facebook group where I talk about secret projects that aren't ready to be shown anywhere else just yet.

You can find all of these places at: lcmawson.com/links

Other Series by L.C. Mawson

Snowverse
Ember Academy for Young Witches
lcmawson.com/emberacademy
Ember Academy for Magical Beings
lcmawson.com/ember-academy-for-magical-beings
Freya Snow – YA/NA Urban Fantasy
lcmawson.com/books/freyasnow
The Royal Cleaner – F/F Urban Fantasy
lcmawson.com/books/the-royal-cleaner
Engineered Rebel – Sci-fi/Urban Fantasy
lcmawson.com/engineered-rebel
Castaway Heart – Mermaid Romance (CW for Steamy Scenes and Domestic Violence)
lcmawson.com/castawayheart
Other
Aspects – YA Sci-fi
lcmawson.com/the-aspects
The Lady Ruth Constance Chapelstone Chronicles – Steampunk Novellas
lcmawson.com/books/ladyruth